I0597178

PATENTLY ABSURD

with

BEN BOWMAN

and

VIOLET

THE FILES OF THE RETROPOLIS REGISTRY OF PATENTS

WRITTEN AND ILLUSTRATED BY BRADLEY W. SCHENCK

PATENTLY ABSURD

"The Purloined Patents of Doctor Brackett", "Doctor Petaja's Parlor of Peril", "Fenwick's Improved Venomous Worms", "Professor Wilcox and the Floating Laboratory", and "Ben Bowman in the Vault of Terror" were serialized, in a slightly different form, at *Thrilling Tales of the Downright Unusual* in 2016 and 2017.

"The Enigma of the Unseen Doctor" appears in this volume for the first time.

Published by Radio Planet Books, 2018
radioplanetbooks.com

ISBN-13: 978-0-9996509-0-5

Book design
by Bradley W. Schenck

CONTENTS

The Purloined Patents of Doctor Brackett

From the files of the Retropolis Registry of Patents

Once the Registrar started playing with his pen, Ben was on familiar ground. The thing about familiar ground, though, is that it's just *familiar*. There are a lot of places that are *familiar*, but which you'd rather not visit again. The new Registrar's pen, when he was playing with it, was the signpost for a place that Ben Bowman knew, and dreaded, and tried to avoid.

Before Mr. Balasco could share his thoughts, Ben leaned forward. "It's not really about the preliminary patent applications. We don't even *need* the preliminary patent applications. We just ask for them so we have some advance warning if, say, some inventor decides to see what happens when you solidify the Earth's core."

Mr. Balasco stared, blankly, the pen now immobile in his fingers.

Ben waited. When waiting didn't help, he explained: "That would be very bad, sir."

"Well, we wouldn't want that, would we? Still, think how much more streamlined the whole process would be if we eliminated those preliminaries, with all their paperwork."

The pen was moving again. Ben tried not to follow it with his eyes.

"But... sir, the whole point of the preliminary applications is that we find out, ahead of time, what the scientists are doing. Before one of them *does* solidify the Earth's core. Which would destroy the magnetic field that holds our atmosphere in place. Which, as I mentioned, sir, would be very bad. Anyway, like I said, it's not really about the preliminary applications. It's about the complaints."

"We've received complaints?"

"As I was just saying, sir. Twenty-seven inventors in the District have lodged complaints against Doctor Brackett. They think she's stolen their ideas, even though they'd already filed their preliminary applications. But in almost every case they've withdrawn their complaints shortly afterward."

Mr. Balasco nodded.

"In three cases the scientists disappeared, sir."

Mr. Balasco put down his pen. "I think you're getting worked up over a very small incident, Ben. Once these complaints were withdrawn, our job was done. And I'm sure you have a lot of other work to do." His fingers strayed over to the pen, and he picked it up again. It started to twirl. "I should think that three fewer scientists in the District would be more a relief, than anything else, anyway."

"Well, I can understand that, sir, but it sets a disturbing precedent. If their little feuds and rivalries should ever flare up into an actual war, then it's likely to spread outside the District. You can't contain the... the giant robots, and the death rays, and the sonic destabilizers they have in there. Not with anything they've invented for us."

Ben waited for that to sink in, which it didn't. "We're here to register their inventions, sir, and that's a great service to the city. Once those new gadgets are licensed and manufactured they're... of considerable benefit. But the thing is – as I think you'll see in your briefing – our first duty is to *contain* the scientists in the District. To prevent their inventions and their arguments from... well, sir, to prevent them from getting out and killing the rest of us. To put it plainly."

"Oh, I've read the briefing," Mr. Balasco said. "*Of course* I've read it."

Ben didn't comment.

"All right, investigate it if you think it's necessary. Naturally I respect your long service and... and your qualifications. Just try to wrap this up quickly, will you?"

The pen was rolling from finger to finger, a disturbing barometer of innovations to come.

"Yes, sir. That's my plan."

Ben nodded to Violet, Mr. Balasco's secretary, as he closed the door. She tilted her enameled head and let one eye dim slightly in a wink. "He's having *ideas*?" she asked.

"The pen."

"I'll take in a stack of reports, then. That'll hold him for the afternoon."

Ben gave her a smile. "Thanks, Violet. That'd be swell."

His smile nearly lasted until he'd reached the boundary of the Experimental Research District, where the mass of Retropolitan pedestrians thinned, quite suddenly, in an illustration of survival instincts at work. It was all laid out in the Zoning regulations, but on a one-to-one level people didn't even need to be told. The frequent explosions were more of a reminder than anybody needed.

Ben stopped across the empty street and steeled himself for the most frightening experience a Patent Registry investigator could face.

The Experimental Research District was one of the largest neighborhoods in all of Retropolis, roughly in the center of the city that sprawled for hundreds of miles in every direction. The District was at once the engine that drove the city and the greatest threat to its safety. The great towers, the monorail system, the lighter-than-air buildings and vehicles could all be traced back to the patented inventions that Ben, and other officers, processed. The District was the source of all that frenetic invention.

It wasn't a lovely neighborhood; it wasn't even slightly attractive, like the neighborhood where Ben lived. The District was a warren of lead-shielded, armored bunkers: of laboratories, in other words. Each scientist lurked behind the reinforced walls that protected their laboratories from the experiments next door, and which might just protect the laboratories next door from what was going on inside. But their defenses weren't perfect. Billowing clouds of fumes often bellied out over the rooftops; there was a nightly light show, with unidentifiable rays shooting out into the clouds – to what effect, no one outside the District could say – and there was also the constant din of construction, since so many laboratories abruptly became steaming craters and were, almost immediately, rebuilt for their new occupants. There was a tremendous amount of turnover in there.

It wasn't a neighborhood that many people would care to join. But the scientists who did live there wouldn't want to live anyplace else. By statute, they *couldn't* live anywhere else. So it worked out pretty well for everyone.

Ben saw a courier fly in on her scooter, keeping to the area directly above the District streets because you didn't want to cause any confusion about the airspace over the laboratories.

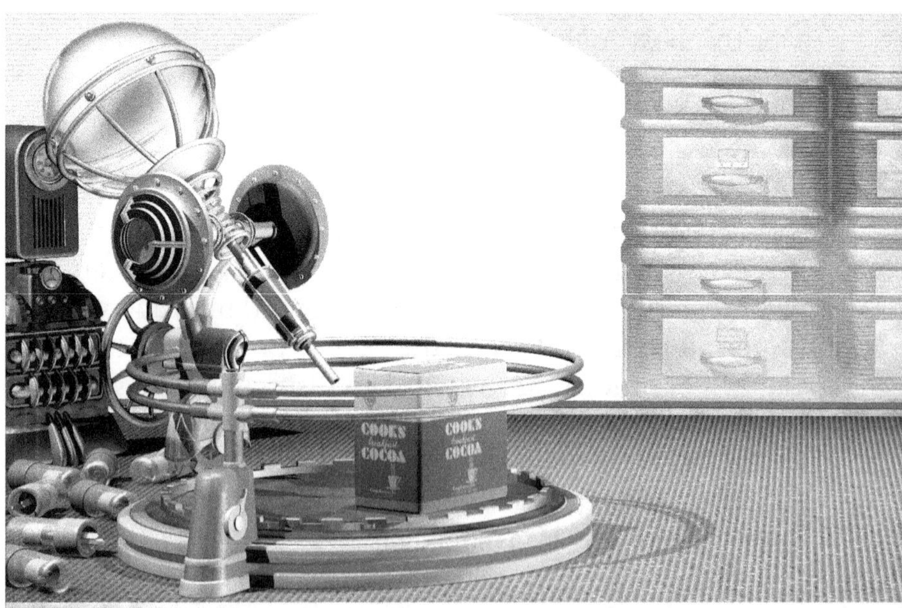

He took a deep breath. Then he crossed the street and took the shortest possible route to Doctor Hamilton's laboratory.

A successful Patent Investigator knew *all* the shortest possible routes.

Doctor Hamilton's laboratory was tucked away on a smoke-stained, pitted street not far from Scarpellini Circle. Like its neighbors, it had several fire escapes – many of them still intact – and a liberal number of vents set deep in its fortified walls. Inside, a dim tiled hallway opened out into several rooms filled with things that Ben preferred not to examine closely.

Among the things that Ben was emphatically not noticing were the loud pumps squatting around a large, glass-walled tank in which something grey and yellow was swimming in short, sudden lunges; a brilliantly glowing set of concentric

tubes that tapered toward a brass cone, aimed at a steel box that was pierced by air holes and which trembled as though it contained something that, like Ben, would rather be elsewhere; and – for no reason that Ben could imagine – an elephant the size of a housecat which trumpeted in a fine alto voice as it sprayed itself with the mud that slurped over the edge of its basin.

Doctor Hamilton had a keen interest in biology.

He was also very friendly with the Patent Registry. But then just about all the District scientists were. The royalties from their inventions were the fuel that propelled their latest research, and their latest research was invariably the thing that brought them joy. Still, Ben declined the doctor's brownies and coffee on general principle and in conformance with Registry Regulation 527b.

He scanned the papers on his clipboard. "It looks like you made a complaint about Doctor Brackett on the twentieth of June, but then on the twenty-third you withdrew your complaint. I'd like to know more about that."

"Oh! Well, that's... that's embarrassing, really," Doctor Hamilton said. He did look a bit sheepish. "It's not unheard of... it's not at all uncommon... I mean, over and over, through history, it turns out that more than one person has made a discovery at about the same time. Some combination of earlier discoveries... some mounting evidence for... well, some things just become more likely. At a certain point a discovery becomes, well, inevitable. And more than one person, working away with the same evidence... well, two people may come to the same conclusion. It happens quite often, I think."

"So you and Doctor Brackett just naturally arrived at the..."

"The hydrostatic re-excitation array."

"The, yes, the hydrostatic re-excitation array, at the same time."

"Well!" Dr Hamilton chuckled. "As it turns out, she was ahead of me on that one, as she demonstrated when I confronted her. Quite... as I said, a bit embarrassing."

Ben turned the page. "And this array has applications in fluid dynamics, as an alternative to mechanical valves?"

"I suppose so, that is, yes, I think it may. But of course it's not... the *practical application*, you could say, is not the point. It's the essential truth of the principle, the idea."

Ben let his eyes wander around Doctor Hamilton's lab. "You've registered thirty-four *essential truths* to date, I believe. And the royalty income from your *essential truths* has enabled you to expand your operation here?"

The scientist blinked. "Well, since you put it that way, let me think, yes, I suppose I've done pretty well... pretty successful, really."

"Pretty profitable. But on the twenty-third of June you decided that you wouldn't contest Doctor Brackett's patent for the *essential truth* of hydrostatic re-excitation."

Something changed in Doctor Hamilton's eyes. He seemed to be looking at something that wasn't in the room. "Well, when I confronted her Doctor Brackett gave me a demonstration of her process. It was... I have to say, it was very complete. Very convincing. Remarkable. And at the end of the demonstration I could see that she had thoroughly researched... that her process was unimpeachable. That she had simply... beaten me to the discovery."

"And can you describe that demonstration for me?"

Ben waited.

"Doctor Hamilton, could you describe Doctor Brackett's demonstration of hydrostatic re-excitation?"

The scientist frowned. "It's highly technical, I'm afraid. It requires a great deal of... it would be difficult to... honestly, I don't see the point. I withdrew the complaint, didn't I? There's nothing to worry about."

"Because the demonstration was so convincing."

"Yes, of course... certainly. Exactly."

This was essentially the same as the Patent officers' reports. In the face of Doctor Brackett's demonstration, they found it obvious that her patent application had been independent. And although she herself had never filed a preliminary application 'due to the sudden nature of the discovery' she'd been granted the patent. In all twenty-seven cases.

"Thank you, Doctor Hamilton. You've been very helpful. Before I go, do you have any preliminary applications I can take back to the office?"

The scientist looked away. "No, not just now. Maybe next week."

Throughout the day Ben carried out eleven other interviews. There wasn't much to choose between them. Each of the eleven scientists had filed a preliminary application, been beaten to the discovery by Doctor Brackett's full application, and filed a complaint; each one of them withdrew the complaint after confronting Doctor Brackett, on the strength of a convincing demonstration that they weren't able or willing to describe. Of the eleven, only three gave him preliminary patent applications to take back to the office.

This was the frightening part of the whole thing, Ben thought. If the District scientists should stop filing their preliminary applications there'd be no way to know what any of them was working on. There would be no way to – carefully, quietly – deflect their research or, in rare cases, take more drastic measures. The entire early warning system of the Patent Registry was in danger.

Ben took the speediest, safest route out of the District and went back to the Patent Registry. He'd have a look at his three preliminary applications and call it a day. Doctor Brackett's interview could wait till tomorrow.

Violet could only blink for effect: she had no eyelids, just those big, lambent lenses set into her rigid face. She blinked now. For effect.

"Nothing to it at all, then?"

Ben grinned. "No, just coincidence. Honestly, Doctor Brackett was amazing – I'd even almost call her sane. She showed me, step by step, how she'd developed the array. Her process was unimpeachable. I just need to tell the Registrar that there's nothing to worry about."

Violet stood and went over to the Registrar's In box. She pulled Ben's report from yesterday and handed it to him.

He gave her a crooked smile. "Yes?"

She pointed at a line near the end of the report. "Could you read me what Doctor Hamilton says there?"

"Her process... was unimpeachable. So?"

"That's exactly what you just said to me. 'Her process was unimpeachable.' And here?"

"There's nothing to worry about."

"Which is what you're about to tell the Registrar."

"That could be a coincidence, though. I mean, it's a common phrase...."

Silently, Violet paged through Ben's other reports from the previous day. Again and again she pointed out the words *her process was unimpeachable* and *there's nothing to worry about*.

Violet sat down again. Her actuators hummed softly as she pulled a patent application out of her typewriter. "Do you remember the three preliminary applications you filed yesterday?"

"Yes, of course. They were, ah, there was... something about morological reversion, and a new way to generate a helical magnetic field, and.... huh. I can't remember that last one."

"It was a method for constructing a gigantic telescope lens in space, by means of suspending beads with a kind of light ray."

Ben laughed. "No, you're all mixed up there. That's the *final* application I brought back today, from Doctor Brackett's laboratory."

He thought for a moment. "Oh. No."

He felt the cool touch of Violet's steel fingers. She was patting him on the hand. "Let's not report this to the Registrar just yet."

"No. Let's not do that just yet," Ben agreed. He sank into Violet's guest chair.

Violet poured a cup of coffee from her urn. He took it, but he wasn't really aware of it until he'd lifted the cup and taken a sip. It was really good coffee.

"It's *us*. She's getting the preliminary applications from *us*. She got one from *me*."

The preliminary patent applications were the Registry's most valuable source of information about research in the District. If this went on, none of the scientists was going to want to file preliminary applications any more: and it was the Patent Registry's own fault. Somehow, they were leaking the preliminaries.

"Violet, could you get me everything we have on Doctor Brackett?"

In the past ten months Doctor Brackett had been granted eighty-three patents. The patents covered a very wide spectrum of invention. That wasn't unusual; the scientists were largely unaware of boundaries between their disciplines. But still, her range of studies was diverse. She'd filed patents on mechanical processes, astronomical observation, biology, subsonic generators, neural analyzers, and propulsion. And all of this, from a scientist whose thesis had been on chronolithic containment. Something about Time?

"And her thesis, Violet, please."

It was pretty dense stuff – all theoretical – but Ben could see that Doctor Brackett had been looking into the possibility of a Time particle, a Chronolith. She'd made a pretty convincing case. It was good enough to land her a doctorate and, eventually, a laboratory in the District. But so far as Ben could see it was all observation and theory, without any practical applications. From that, she'd somehow become a modern da Vinci with patents in just about every field of study.

Ben went back to her file. After her graduation she'd served for a year as Professor Fenwick's laboratory assistant. Then she'd somehow managed to establish her own lab.

Ben's third cup of coffee had gone cold, he discovered. "Professor Fenwick," he said aloud.

Violet, typing away at the desk next to him, said "Terribly

sad, with him so young."

"It really was a mystery, too. I mean, there he is, researching dreams, and the next thing you know his whole laboratory turns into a carnivorous fungus. No way out, of course."

He thought back to the incident. "We all figured it was due to something Doctor Pratt was doing next door. With the biomass dispersal system. Some kind of accident. But it was so much like a nightmare that you had to wonder whether he'd done it himself, somehow. With his dream research."

Violet spun a letter out of her typewriter and set it aside. A blank sheet of paper rolled into its place. "Doctor Brackett must have been very fortunate," she said. "To be out running an errand at the time."

Very fortunate. Time, and dreams.

"Do you have dreams, Violet?"

The typing stopped.

"I have aspirations," she said at last.

"No, but, you know, when you sleep. Do you dream when you're asleep?" It was something he'd never considered.

"I don't sleep. Not exactly, not the way human people do. It's different for us."

"But…."

"No, I don't dream when I'm sleeping. I'm happy with my aspirations."

"If I ask the Registrar, do you think he'd loan you to me tomorrow? For a little field work?"

Violet struck seven keys with an unusual amount of force. "I'm not a briefcase," she told him.

"No, I… what I meant was, I…."

They looked at each other over the silent typewriter.

"If you ask me, I might be able to arrange it," she said. "In view of my aspirations."

"That would be great. Uh, would you come with me tomorrow to the District?"

"Yes, that would be nice," she said. "If I wait until he's overdue for his nap I can't see any difficulty."

"Overdue...?"

"I handed him three months' worth of expense projections this morning. I had a feeling we'd want him to be malleable."

"Violet. You're amazing."

"It's kind of you to say so," she observed from behind her typewriter.

"But... how did you know? This morning?"

"I'm amazing," she said, and she went back to typing a letter for the Registrar.

It took a little longer to reach Doctor Brackett's laboratory the next morning. There was a breakout along Chien-Shiung Way that blocked several of the adjacent streets with packs of small, ravenous creatures who looked like a cross between an armadillo and a snail. They were surprisingly fast, as Ben learned when Violet whipped him out of their way. Anyhow all the neighborhood inventors were out on their porches and stoops, each armed with something that was arguably more dangerous than a snailadillo.

As always, this led to some cross-disciplinary disagreements. The whole affair stopped just short of a riot, and after half an hour Ben and Violet were able to crawl out of the crater where they'd taken shelter. Their way was nearly clear; they were only attacked by one more viscous, armored pack on their way. The sidewalks, unfortunately, were now coated with slime and shell fragments and the remains of every anti-snailadillo countermeasure that had been brought to bear, including one *actual* bear with something like a colander strapped to its cranium.

"Your first time?" Ben asked.

"Oh, no," Violet told him. "I've been here before."

Doctor Brackett met them at the door, smiling and friendly. Ben introduced Violet as his assistant and they were led in.

The Brackett laboratory was unusually... tidy, Ben thought. All her experiments were divided by discipline on orderly tables; maybe that's why there seemed to be so few of them. Normally there would be a frantic and dangerous clutter with little regard for the effects of one experiment on the ones to either side. This was a part of the reason Ben had come to think of Doctor Brackett as unusually sane.

"Some problem with the new application?"

They had settled into a kind of nook near a kitchen area – the lab's only kitchen, probably – and Ben had, as usual, declined the tea and cakes Doctor Brackett offered. He'd warned Violet to avoid the three-weight oil, too.

"Just a few things that weren't quite clear. About those light rays and the, uh, the telescope."

Doctor Brackett rose to adjust a standing lamp that was directed at the couch where Ben and Violet were sitting. Her hand lingered on a dial near its shade.

"I'm sure we can clear that up," she said. "What exactly did you want to –"

On their way down the steps, Ben laughed to himself. "I can't believe we were so suspicious," he said. "When there's nothing..."

"...to worry about?" Violet finished.

He stopped so suddenly that he nearly tripped. "Jeepers."

They turned back to look at the façade of Doctor Brackett's reinforced bunker.

"So..." he started, after a moment. "Once we sat down, what do you...."

"We spoke for a moment, she got up, and thirty-two milliseconds later we were walking down the steps."

They looked around. Whatever had happened, they were still in the middle of the Experimental Research District and in that situation the best plan was to get out, as quickly as

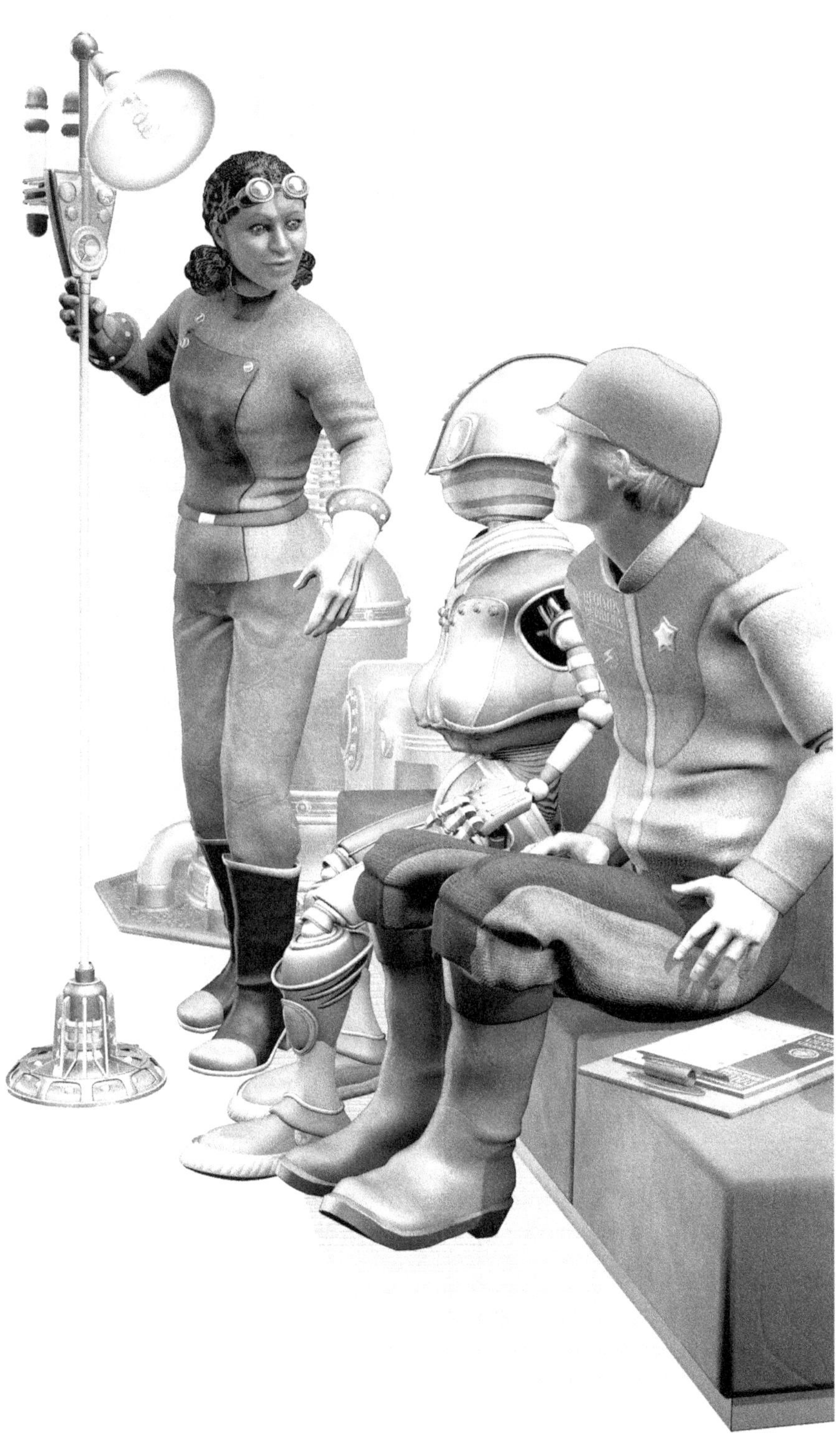

possible. They hurried between the squatting rows of laboratories.

"Do you think she knows what you remember?" Ben asked.

"We can't be sure," Violet said. "I think it might be extremely dangerous to ask her."

"I was hoping that you'd be immune to whatever she's doing."

"Maybe I am," Violet said. They rounded a corner and stepped out of the way of the bear, who was still roaming freely. The colander on the bear's head was sparking now with big, green sparks that seemed to be looking for something. "I don't have the same false memories that you have. But I can't remember anything else, either."

"When we get back to the office I want you to check your internal clock against, I don't know, all the other clocks? To see if you're missing any time."

"I'm not," she said. "I've already checked against the readings of the Time Reference Bureau."

"So it starts with Time," Ben decided. "She's doing something outside of the flow of Time."

"If she's outside the normal flow of Time there's no mystery about how she develops those preliminary reports into full patent applications. Apparently she can have all the time she needs, squeezed into thirty-two milliseconds."

They could just see the safety of the Street of Wings in the distance.

"Then the other thing is the memories," Ben said. "And my bet is that she's developed Professor Fenwick's dream research into a way to create them."

"Yes, naturally."

Ben glared at her. "Naturally? Really?"

"It's probably a little harder for you," Violet said. "You've been… intruded on. You're having an emotional reaction to what she did to you."

They pressed on. Only one more block to go.

"And I suppose you *don't* have emotional reactions?"

"You've *met* the Registrar, haven't you?"

Ben grunted. Then he came to a stop and grabbed her by one arm.

"Say, wait. What if we build some kind of Farraday cage around your head? You know, so your brain and your eyes are separate from your body. Inside the cage. I could, like, wheel your head around on a dolly. That way you might be protected from whatever she did to us, like, uh, like an electromagnetic field effect, and you can explain it to me after."

Violet removed his hand from her arm.

"Oh, or even better!" she said brightly. "What if we extract your *brain* and encant it into a *tube?* Suspended in solution inside that thick glass, your neural processes might be isolated from Doctor Brackett's effect. And then *you* can explain it to *me*."

He stared at her.

"They're doing wonderful things with those tubes, lately. They can even put your brain on a little motorized cart. There's a choice of sensory apparatus."

"I...."

She waited.

"Okay," he said. "Point taken. No Farraday cage."

"Are you sure? Those little brain carts are *very* sporty."

"Sorry. Really. Meant no offense."

"I know."

"But somehow, we need to get around whatever it was she did to us."

They started down the street again. Safety was just ahead.

"When we get back to the office I'll make a pot of coffee, Ben. That seems to keep you on track."

It was just an idea, Ben thought. *The Farraday cage. No need to get all sensitive about it.* But, wisely, he said nothing.

"A hidden camera?" Ben tried. "Something that would record her while she... implants... those memories?"

"Maybe."

Violet was catching up on her typing. They were ignoring the Registrar's snores, just audible through his office door. She rolled out a letter and replaced it with a blank sheet of paper.

"He sure has a lot of correspondence," Ben observed. What could he possibly be writing about? The man just napped and had inane ideas.

"He has a lot of ideas about City Management," Violet said. "I've been encouraging him to share as many of them as possible. He's up to six or seven a day, now."

Ben poured himself another cup of coffee. "Six or seven a day?" He thought about all those letters spreading Balasco's ideas through the system. "Yeah, I can see how that might work. But aren't we *better off* with this sleepyhead? You never know what a new Registrar would be like."

Violet paused to check her flawlessly justified address block. "He's told me he won't ever consider promoting a secretary into the Investigators' Department."

Ben drank his coffee. He thought about it. "That would be one of your *aspirations*?"

She didn't answer.

"When does he have the time to dictate the letters?" Ben asked. "I mean...." He pointed at the door. A particularly loud snore was making it shake, ever so slightly.

"I'm helping him with that," Violet told him. "This one, for example, is a letter I'm sending to the Retropolis Department of Power & Light. It's about changing the color of all their street lamps every week, to encourage productivity."

Ben stared at her.

"Uh, Violet, I hope that if you ever, you know, if I should ever annoy you in some way...."

She kept typing until she reached the signature; then she whirled the sheet off and replaced it with a new blank. "You'll know."

Ben was pretty sure that he'd know, all right. He was thinking about the last couple of Registrars. It seemed like they hadn't lasted very long, either.

"I'm afraid that a camera may not work," Violet said. "Her process, or her device, or her machine... it only seems to work on human beings. A camera would probably just skip thirty-two milliseconds, and that would be that. We wouldn't know unless we tried, of course. But I don't think we should count on it."

Ben had to agree that this was likely.

"There has to be *something,*" he said. "If this goes on, there's no way to know what she'll do. She could conceal anything from us. She could... she could manipulate us in any way she chose."

Violet seemed absorbed by the blank sheet of paper in her typewriter. "That *would* be terrible."

"I've got those royalty statements from her accountant. She's made an incredible amount of money in the past year. It's just going to keep on building with every new patent she registers. I've gotta say, if we don't stop her now it's possible that we won't *ever* stop her. Look at what she did to those other scientists, the ones who didn't drop their complaints."

"I can't look at that," Violet said. She crossed her enameled arms across her chest. "We have no idea what she did to them."

"My point."

Ben went back to the royalty statements. It was a lot of money. Meanwhile, Violet had finished her letters and was starting on the envelopes.

She seemed to have a thought. Ben saw that she'd half-rolled an envelope onto the roller. Her eyes were fixed on its upper edge, just peeking out above the platen.

"What is it?" he asked.

"Don't you...?"

"Don't I what?"

Violet turned to face him. "I've read your file. I know your background. I'm just wondering whether... whether any of your *connections* might be of help. From your old life."

Ben could swear that she was blushing, even though he knew that wasn't possible.

"You had a Professor...."

"Zappencackler." Ben frowned. He was fighting an urge to get out of there. "You read my file."

"I read *all* the files."

"Yeah, okay, my background, it's unusual," he said. "I guess you think...."

And then *he* thought.

"Oh, I see," he said. "Yeah, you might be right. We're not the only ones who are at risk, here."

Violet rolled the envelope through the platen. "I'm sorry, Ben. I know it's not my business."

"It's okay."

He jumped out of his chair, barely saving his coffee, and kissed the top of her head.

On his way through the door he heard her say, "That's *quite inappropriate,* Investigator."

Violet finished the first envelope, so she rolled it out and reached for the next while she hummed, very softly, to herself.

Cornelius Zappencackler was as big a fish as you could find in the District. He'd filed a prestigious number of patents, most of them profitable, and in addition to that he taught at the Retropolis Academy for the Unusually Inventive. Inasmuch as any scientist listened to any other scientist, he was listened to. He was always strangely pleased to see Ben.

Ben violated Regulation 527b by taking the bottom scone from the plate the Professor offered him.

Professor Zappencackler smiled. "Very good! Avoid the top one," he said. "We're always short of experimental subjects around here."

Ben got directly to the point. He laid out what he knew, and what he suspected, and what he thought they might do about it.

The Professor shared Ben's concern. "That could lead to all sorts of problems. I know you worry about the rest of the city, but if my colleagues found that they were being swindled by Doctor Brackett we might see an all-out war erupt here in the District. And, of course, your other fears are well grounded too. I'm glad you brought this to me."

"Do you have something that fits the bill?" Ben asked.

"Yes, I think so." The Professor chewed a bite of the *second* scone from the top. "You always were a bright student, Ben. Your other teachers were confused when your test scores came back so badly. Badly, I mean, in a way that's so unlikely, statistically."

"It's not for everyone, sir," Ben said.

"Oh, certainly not. I'm sure you're far happier where you are. Do you have that form for me?"

It was unusual, but not unheard of, for a patent registration to be delivered personally. What Doctor Brackett couldn't know was that it would never be an Investigator who made that kind of delivery.

"I see you've left your charming assistant behind," she said.

"Yes, Violet's quite busy today. And anyway, this is just routine."

Ben handed Doctor Brackett the patent. "This one's pretty

remarkable," he said. "They'll be able to build a telescope as wide as... as wide as the orbit of Venus. Or, you know, whatever size they want."

"Oh, there will be limits," said Doctor Brackett. "There are always limits. That's how people like me stay in business, isn't it? Here, please have a seat."

Ben sat on the couch at the end farthest from Doctor Brackett's curious floor lamp. He set down his clipboard with its single preliminary patent application while Doctor Brackett wandered over to the lamp and reached for the dial.

A minute or so later Violet, Professor Zappencackler, and Zappencackler's young assistant broke down the laboratory door. They found Ben seated on the couch, bathed by the eerie blue rays of the floor lamp. Violet was the first to reach the lamp. She turned its dial down, slowly, and the blue rays grew fainter until they had disappeared.

Ben remained unresponsive for a moment, but at last he blinked twice and wiped his forehead. "Did it work?" he asked.

Violet pointed down the hall. "They're looking for her now," she said.

Ben got up and the two of them went looking for Professor Zappencackler.

They found him, standing with his assistant, in one of Doctor Brackett's workrooms. There was a lot of electrical apparatus arranged on two of the tables, with a bank of red lights, a bank of green lights, and three peculiar control panels that seemed, somehow, not to be entirely there.

Doctor Brackett was suspended in the air between the banks of lights. There was something wrong with the texture of her skin (scales) and most of her hair had disappeared (feathers). Her legs had shrunken considerably, and her face....

Ben hoped that someday he'd be able to forget about her face.

"Lew," said the Professor, one hand on his assistant's shoulder. "Could you gather her up? We probably won't need the...."

He pointed down. Ben hoped he'd be able forget what he saw there, too.

Lew started to bundle up what had recently been Doctor Brackett.

The Professor turned to Ben. "Really, quite a remarkable result," he said. He seemed very pleased. "She'll furnish us with weeks of study."

"So..." Ben kept his eyes on Zappencackler. "I guess that's what you, uh, expected?"

"Oh, hardly! Half the time we don't know *what* to expect. That's what makes this so *exciting*."

"So when you filled out that preliminary patent application...."

Violet stepped up next to him. "You mean you didn't even know what would happen to her when she tried to complete the experiment? That seems... so risky."

The Professor looked from her to Ben. "You should bring your friends around more often, Ben. No, young lady, I didn't know *exactly* what would happen. But I did know that twelve different aspects of this experiment would be very harmful to any carbon-based life form that attempted it. Honestly, she got much farther than I could have dreamed."

He seemed to disapprove of something in the area of the room that Ben wasn't looking at. "No, Lew! Use the *bucket!* Why do you think we brought the *bucket?*"

He shook his head. "Assistants these days. I don't know what to tell you. Anyway, no human being could complete that experiment before it, heh heh, completed *her*. And that, as you can see, is all I needed to know. Don't you agree?"

RETROPOLIS
REGISTRY
OF PATENTS
OFFICE OF THE
REGISTRAR

Back at the Patent Registry, Ben and Violet sank back into their normal tasks, hoping that somehow their routine would help them forget the penultimate fate of Doctor Brackett. Not her ultimate fate; *that* would be starting, right about now, in the dim tiled rooms of Zappencackler's laboratory. What they already knew was more than enough.

The Registrar wasn't able to receive their report, though. He'd been called to an urgent meeting by thirteen different department heads in City Government.

Ben leaned back with his coffee. Violet was idling, too; her typing chores seemed to be complete.

"This could be it," he said, and toasted her with his coffee cup. "Could be the last day of Mr. Sleepyhead."

The Registrar's door was hanging open.

"Oh, it is," she told him. When he raised an eyebrow she admitted that there was a lot of informative interchange between secretaries.

"So you'll be hoping that the new Registrar is more receptive to those aspirations of yours."

"Well, there's always hope," Violet said. "But I've found it's more useful to take an active stance."

"I'll put in a word..."

"Oh, that's very thoughtful of you."

"...if you need it."

She looked back calmly – or so he supposed – and glanced at the coffeepot. "More?"

"I'll make it," he said quickly. "You just... you just relax." He got up and opened up the coffeemaker.

"It was very brave, what you did," she said behind him. "I was a little worried about you."

"Thanks."

And then they just sat and waited for the news that they were getting a new Patent Registrar.

WHICH OF YOUR FRIENDS STAYS AT
TUBULAR BELLE'S?
YOU CAN'T TELL. WE WON'T SAY.
Enjoy the best, most affordable accommodations the city has to offer, with perfect confidence in our discretion. Nobody knows, except... your banker!

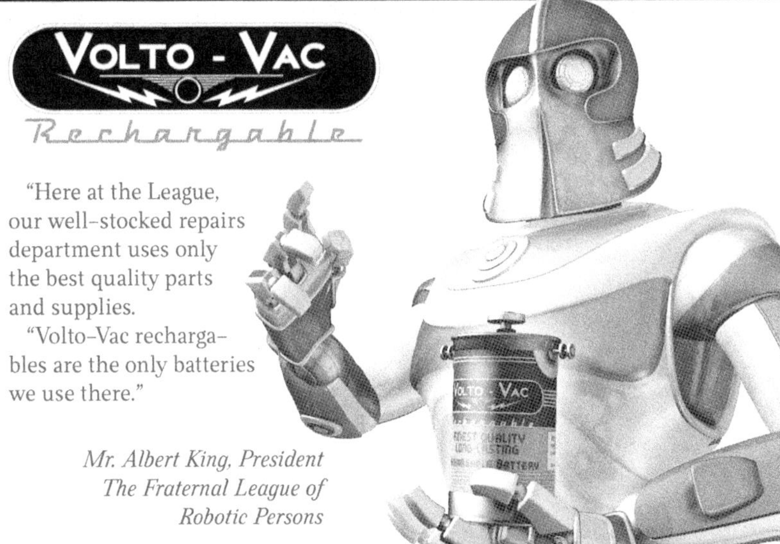
THE FRATERNAL LEAGUE OF ROBOTIC PERSONS
VOLTO - VAC
Rechargable
"Here at the League, our well-stocked repairs department uses only the best quality parts and supplies.
"Volto-Vac rechargables are the only batteries we use there."
Mr. Albert King, President
The Fraternal League of Robotic Persons
BUYS OUR BATTERIES BY THE CRATE
AND THEY'RE THE PEOPLE WHO KNOW THEIR BATTERIES

Smoky Craters
STEAK SAUCE
You'll think you just ate the wrong side of Mercury

VULCAN
ALL YOUR CLOTHES
SONICLAVE
FRESH &
CLEAN BY
MORNING

Doctor Petaja's Parlor Of Peril

It was hard to figure, how a robot could brew the best coffee in the office when she never drank the stuff herself. But Ben had stopped wondering about that. He poured himself a cup while he didn't look at the new Registrar's office door. It was closed, anyway.

"She working out?" he asked. "I only ask 'cause, you know, I've been kind of busy."

Violet looked up from her filing. The Registry of Patents sometimes seemed like one big operation that simply moved folders from one cabinet to another. If you ignored the casualties.

"She's a little frustrated by the lack of qualified candidates."

This was because, when it came down to it, you *couldn't* ignore the casualties. Registrar Finlay had begun her reign with an attempt at a hiring spree that might have swelled the ranks of Patent Officers and Investigators with fresh, optimistic faces. It had seemed like a good plan, especially to the new Registrar. It just wasn't working out that way.

Ben wandered over to Violet, whose enameled face was once again buried in the filing drawers. She had these little rubber sleeves on the tips of her steely fingers. Ben sipped his coffee. "You're refiling the old registrations?"

Violet's head bobbed, but she didn't bother to explain.

"Only, I don't quite get the system. They're...."

"In reverse alphabetical order," she told him.

He was wondering whether he should ask when a stranger in a brand new uniform came through the door and actually saluted.

Violet closed the file cabinet and gave the new recruit a look. "Officer Binder."

"Present and correct, ma'am. Ready for my first assignment."

"You've read the regulations?"

"Yes, ma'am."

"You've had your briefing?"

Officer Binder hesitated. "We had that meeting this morning, with a short instructional film...."

"But nobody sat you down and had a talk with you?"

"Uh...."

"They must be very busy. Well, you should make your rounds, and if you're confused about anything you can aways talk to Mr. Bowman here. He's a very experienced investigator."

"Oh, I know, ma'am! Investigator Bowman, he's what you call a legendary character."

The legendary character made humble noises and smiled. Then Officer Binder decided to shake his hand, and he went along with it. There was one of those awkward moments while he and Violet waited for the youngster to figure out that they were done with him, but eventually he caught on and he went.

"He looks familiar," Ben said.

"Mail room. Two years."

"He came up from the mail room? She's promoting from within! You should – "

Violet, with a fresh stack of files, looked up and stared at him.

Ben hid behind his coffee. But having come so far, he had to keep going.

"So she won't make you an investigator. Fair enough – she doesn't even know you. Did you apply to be a Patent Officer?"

"Yes, I was that desperate. But no. She's won't consider promoting a secretary."

"Look, I can put in a word. She probably has no idea – "

"That's very kind, Ben. But you know I prefer to handle things my own way." Violet slid open another file drawer and went back to her reverse alphabetical filing.

Ben thought it over. "Yeah, I guess I can see that."

His eyes wandered over to the Registrar's door. They never lasted very long, the Registrars. Somehow, once they'd denied Violet the promotion she wanted, they never hung around much longer.

"Shame, really. I had hopes for this one."

But it was time Ben got on with his day. He thanked Violet for the coffee, which was a sensible thing to do, and he shuffled through the papers on his clipboard so he could plan the shortest possible route through the Experimental Research District. This was also a sensible thing to do.

You don't last long at the Registry of Patents without being sensible. Also, there's luck. You can't deny the importance of luck.

To an outsider, the Experimental Research District might seem like a peculiar institution, though it's less like an institution than a neighborhood. It was established so long ago by the zoning regulations of Retropolis that it has become an institution over time.

The idea is simple; the solution, ingenious.

When a society is faced with the rapid growth of technological progress there's a lot to celebrate: the lighter than air metals, the mysterious rays, the advanced robotics, and the unexpected sources of energy, all originating in the District, are a clear benefit to the city of Retropolis. One could make the argument – if it were needed – that the city wouldn't even exist if not for the constant, furious inventive powerhouse of the District scientists.

But if those scientists were spread carelessly around the city, the city might not exist for very long.

In some universes scientists may be careful, methodical researchers who work under rigorously controlled conditions and who seldom, if ever, decide to find out what happens when you cross a great white shark with a lawnmower, and then add a rocket pack. That is not the case here.

Some early critics of the zoning regulations questioned the wisdom of crowding all the city's scientists into a single neighborhood. The answer – which proved to be correct – was that when their laboratories exploded, melted, transformed into glowing jelly, or decided suddenly that they ought to exist four doors down, they would *only destroy the laboratories of other scientists*. The city that surrounded them would not be affected. Not in most cases.

The other argument – that crowding the scientists together might lead to a united force that could overcome the rest of the city – was also easily disproved by the tendency of scientists to be highly competitive, distrustful, and energetic.

So in every way it was safer, for most people, to confine all scientific research to a single neighborhood.

The District wasn't visited by emergency services or by most civilians. It was a kind of anarchic, kingless tribe in the middle of the city. But it wasn't completely unsupervised.

That was the mission of the Registry of Patents.

Ben and Doctor Petaja were alone in the laboratory, technically, but Ben couldn't shake the sense that he was being observed by the twelve immobile robots that formed a circle around the parlor. Their eyes were dark, and their actuators were silent. Ben knew they were inactive. But they *stared*.

Doctor Petaja seemed to be completely unaware of them. "It's always a pleasure to see you, Investigator. It's just that I'm not sure why you've come. Cookie?"

Ben declined with a smile. Under Regulation 527b he was forbidden to accept any food or drink while he was on duty.

He didn't mind: he understood why. So did the scientists, of course, but they couldn't ignore the opportunity. Experimental subjects were difficult to locate by conventional means.

He lifted his clipboard, weighed down as it was by seventy-two preliminary patent applications. "Officer Ennis was concerned about the number of preliminary applications you filed yesterday. It's... unusual."

"Oh, pish," said the scientist. "My mind is highly active, and the Essential Neural Energizer has made it unnecessary for me to sleep. I've been extremely productive this week. I hope I haven't caused you any difficulty?"

"Not a bit, sir. I'm happy for you – if even half of these turn into something useful, well, your royalties are going to go right through the roof."

Ben didn't mention that he couldn't see a lot of commercial application for the *Enhanced Method of Air Expulsion for Cetaceans*. That one wasn't a worry, of course; not like the *Proposed Technique for Liquefying Cellular Material By Means Of Distant Modified Rainfall*. Whatever that one was, it sounded like trouble.

He shifted in his chair, hiding his face from six of the lifeless robots. The dark eyes of the other six were also aimed right at him. "No, sir, it's just that Officer Ennis wasn't able to get through the entire stack of preliminaries, so he called me in. I just thought we should meet so you'd know what was going on. But the preliminary applications are all filed and on record, sir. Nothing to worry about there."

Doctor Petaja seemed pleased. "I should have a few dozen more by the end of the week, Investigator."

"So, uh, does that mean that you're not going ahead with these, then?"

"Not at all! Expect several of the final applications at the same time."

It was possible that everything here was exactly as Doctor Petaja claimed. Ben had read the final patent application for the Essential Neural Energizer. If you don't mind the aftereffects, the device could certainly let you work 'round the clock for weeks at a time. So maybe the scientist was telling the plain truth, and he'd just gotten so productive that he was inventing himself into the next century.

It was another possibility that worried Ben, and this was the reason why Officer Ennis had handed him the case. It might just be that Doctor Petaja had figured out the real reason for the preliminary applications – the real purpose of the Registry of Patents – and that seventy-one of these preliminary applications were meant to disguise the danger posed by the seventy-second. There was nothing in Doctor Petaja's manner to tell Ben, one way or the other. So he'd have to head back to the office and explore every one of these preliminaries with great caution.

"Well, you've certainly done the right thing," he said. "With these preliminaries on file, no one else in the District should be able to steal a march on you in, uh, seventy-two cases. Your inventions should be completely secure."

"Thanks so much, Investigator. You're always very helpful."

Ben rose and adjusted his cap. He'd be glad to get away from those twelve motionless robots. "Till next time, then," he smiled. Doctor Petaja showed him out.

"The whales will definitely be excited about this one," Violet observed. She was reading *Enhanced Method of Air Expulsion for Cetaceans.*

Ben looked up from *Certain Unusual Applications for Magnetism with Regard to the Disembodiment of the Currently Embodied.* "Yeah, okay, but picture every one of those whales with, say, an explosive charge stuck in its blowhole. Then what do you get? "

"An extremely unlikely outcome," Violet replied. "Though it's true that they live a long time and have very good memories. There used to be a lot of whaling."

It *was* kind of a stretch, Ben admitted.

Registrar Finlay came out of her office. "I can't seem to find the file on Doctor Brackett," she said.

Violet pointed at the end of the row of cabinets. "The B's are second from the end."

The Registrar looked at Violet, and then at the cabinets. "I see."

She walked over to the B Cabinet and extracted a file. Then she walked upstream, as it were, and pulled one from the G's.

"Reverse alphabetical?"

"It puts the Z's right next to your office door," Violet explained. "And the Z's, of course, are vital."

"Oh, yes," the Registrar agreed. "We can't forget Professor Zardoz."

"Much as we might wish to," Violet agreed.

Ben nodded. The Registrar took the files back into her office. A moment later, her head popped out from behind the door. "Are you assisting Investigator Bowman again?"

Ben tried not to squirm. "Uh, during a lull in her duties, Violet is helping me read through a large number of preliminaries."

Violet turned expectantly toward the door. "Did you need me, Registrar?"

"It's just that I'm so impressed with our new filing system. I wonder, though.... Wouldn't it be better to arrange A–M in reverse alphabetical order, and then N–Z in, ah, *normal* alphabetical? That would put the M's in easy reach. I'm quite interested in the M's."

She retreated into her office. Ben and Violet stared at the door.

"Hey," Ben whispered. "She's pretty good."

Violet didn't answer. She just headed toward the file cabinets.

"Any news about the new kid?" he asked. "Only, he should

have been back by now, and it's his first day."

"No word from the front," Violet told him, She was holding the entire stack of A files in both hands.

"You need a hand with those?" he asked.

"Oh, no. I'll be fine."

Ben had separated Doctor Petaja's seventy-two preliminaries into three piles: *Apparently Harmless* on the left; *Mildly Concerning* in the middle; and *Possibly Dangerous* on the right. It had been a long day. He was nearly at the end of it.

The third pile was the smallest. *Proposed Technique for Liquefying Cellular Material By Means Of Distant Modified Rainfall* was on top of that one.

"Investigator Bowman?"

He looked up and saw Officer Binder in the doorway. "Come in, come in," he waved. Officer Binder didn't take a chair.

"How was your first day?"

"Just fine, sir. I understand that they want us to be... cautious, and all, and I guess I was expecting all kinds of trouble. But it was smooth as... smooth as anything, sir."

"Good to hear it," Ben told him. "But don't get relaxed out there. You read the regulations?"

Officer Binder nodded. "Oh, sure," he said. "You bet."

"Could you turn your head to the left, Binder?"

Ben looked closely at a spot behind Binder's ear. "And to the right?"

Officer Binder complied.

"You have any trouble with your hearing?"

"No, sir."

"Oh. Well, that's good, then."

It was probably better to leave it alone. "Well, have a good evening, Binder. Make sure you get your rest."

"Yes, sir. Thank you, sir."

Ben watched the recruit as he went out the door and down the hall. He had *said* he read the regulations. Chances were, it was nothing.

Was there some hidden danger in Petaja's *Completely Revised Application of Highly Energized Light Rays in the Analysis of Atmospheric Composition*? It seemed so innocent, really: just a way to detect impurities in the air. Probably. Ben switched on his desk lamp and started to go through the left-hand pile another time.

"At this rate," he told Violet over his morning coffee, "Doctor Petaja will have filed another six dozen preliminary applications before I've finished with the ones I have already."

When he turned to look her way the robot secretary was sweeping a pile of papers into her wastebasket.

She looked up. "I was a little concerned about *Certain Unusual Applications for Magnetism*. But I think it might be a red herring."

"Yeah, my thought too. So obvious. But still...."

"If he's really burying us in the paperwork he's quite resourceful. I don't think it's ever been done before."

"Nope. I thought the same thing. But honestly, you know the files better than me."

"Yes, the files," she said. "The files."

"You all done with the refiling?"

"I am."

"Only I noticed you throwing away some papers, just then. You wouldn't...."

"*Investigator!* I would *never*."

"No, sure, of course. Just one of those idle thoughts."

The Registrar came out of her office. "Violet, I need you to take a letter."

Once they were gone, Ben happened to look into the

wastebasket. There were seven applications there: not patent applications, because of course Violet would *never;* these were employment applications. Ben paged through them. Some of these applicants sounded pretty good. They all wanted to be investigators, he noticed. No wonder the Registry was promoting kids out of the mail room, if all the applications were....

He just managed to get them back into the wastebasket before Violet made it through the door. She eyed him, a suspicious gleam in her lenses.

Ben sipped his coffee. "This is sure good," he said. She sat behind her desk and rolled a sheet of paper into the typewriter.

"Was there anything else?"

He wasn't hurt, though she was being short with him. You just had to know Violet.

"Not a thing. Thanks for the coffee."

Ben had started a fourth pile, in one corner of his desk. He thought of this one as *Really Strange*.

The only one of Doctor Petaja's applications that had made it to that pile was *Enhanced Method of Air Expulsion for Cetaceans.*

Now, Ben knew that you couldn't expect a lot of what you'd call *sense* out of the District scientists. Their research tended to evolve in outrageous patterns that were bounded only by what the scientists had been thinking about recently. It didn't really matter whether these things had commercial applications. They just had to be really interesting to a person who had the right sort of mind. Still, why would anyone be interested in creating more efficient blowholes for whales?

He wanted to ask Violet about that, but they'd parted on that odd note this morning. Maybe later. He looked back at the *Mildly Concerning* pile. If it was him, that's where the bombshell would be hidden. In the middle of things that seemed pretty much harmless, touched with the slightest flavor of... ominosity? Which is to say, *perfectly average* preliminary patent applications. If you wanted to hide something, that's where it would go.

"'Morning, Investigator Bowman."

It sounded like Officer Binder. Ben just waved without looking up. He heard the new officer make his way down the hall, a "Good morning" for everybody. Nice kid.

Was there some reason Ben had been thinking about him? He shook his head. Probably. But it wasn't important right now.

Ben could sense Doctor Petaja's new stack of preliminary

applications out there, poised to strike in just a few more days. It felt pretty much like sitting in the middle of the mad doctor's circle of robots. Like something was watching you, even when nothing was really there.

He thought about that for a moment. Could be, that's all it was: maybe the super-energized scientist was simply cranking out a big batch of inventions for as long as he could, until he finally collapsed from the effects of his Essential Neural Energizer. Could be all it was.

Still, it was the responsibility of the Registry of Patents, and of its officers and investigators, to make *sure* that was all it was.

Ben longed for another cup of coffee. But the coffee in the cafeteria was pretty terrible, and he wanted to stay out of Violet's way for, oh, another sixteen hours or so.

He sighed. It wasn't any picnic, being a Patent Investigator. Maybe Violet was doing those applicants a favor by tossing their résumés in the trash.

At the day's end Ben was still moving Doctor Petaja's preliminary applications from one stack to another, and then – usually – back again. He was staring at *Proposed Technique for Liquefying Cellular Material By Means Of Distant Modified Rainfall* when he heard some kind of uproar out in the hall.

It was bound to be more interesting, whatever it was. He ambled out into a close huddle of officers, investigators, and secretaries – with a friendly nod to Violet – and at its center he found Officer Binder, looking a bit embarrassed.

Officer Binder had what sure looked like a pair of frog's legs sticking out of his head, one behind each ear. "They just sort of popped up," the young man was saying. "Like pimples, really. I don't think it's anything, you know, to be worried about."

Violet was staring at his frog's legs.

Now, one problem in dealing with mechanical persons is that none of the usual nonverbal cues are there. A robot might be laughing, or consumed with worry, or could be – and, often enough, was – thinking about last night's chess tournament at Chatrang Stadium. You had to really get to know an individual robot to read the body language. Even then, it was kind of a crapshoot.

But Ben had been drinking Violet's coffee regularly. So when he looked at her right now, what he saw was guilt. It was written all over her slumped shoulders, the way she held her hands, and the slightly dimmed glow of her eyes.

He forced his way through the crowd and had a look behind the new guy's ears. "Well, they're not pimples," he said. "They sure ain't pimples."

He recalled that the new officer had had those green spots behind his ears, just the other night. And now....

"Okay, buddy. You're going to be fine. Now, you had your orientation just the other day, right? And they gave you the regulation book. I remember. When you read the book, you read Regulation 527b?"

Officer Binder looked lost. "That was... Always Avoid Violating Laboratory Airspace? No! That one was, ah, Procedure For Requesting Laboratory Egress...?"

Ben and Violet traded a look. "Regulation 527b," said Ben, "forbids you from accepting gifts of food or drink from any District scientist. No cookies, cakes or pies; no sandwiches or any other food or drink while on the premises. You never, ever, eat or drink anything they give you."

There was a brief silence.

"Even macaroons?"

"Doctor Isip," said Violet. "We sent him to collect Doctor Isip's preliminaries on his first day."

Collectively, the crowd of people groaned or gulped. Doctor Isip's macaroons were a well known hazard at the Registry.

IT HAS BEEN
0173
DAYS
Incident

"Get him to the Infirmary," Ben said, and three officers took Binder in hand and led him down the hall.

The group slowly faded away into their offices. On her way past the '173 Days Since an Incident' sign, Officer Fearn flipped the number over to zero.

Ben and Violet looked at the sign.

Without a word, they went back to Violet's desk outside the Registrar's door. Ben sat down in her guest chair while Violet opened up the coffeepot and did whatever special, unique thing it was that she did to the office coffee.

"You can't blame yourself," Ben told her. "He was warned. He just didn't pay attention."

"They were shorthanded that morning," she said, "due to there being so few investigators on duty. He didn't have the briefing."

Ben looked at the wastebasket, then away.

"Still not your fault," he said. "Everyone knows, they get the briefing before they go out there."

Violet started her mysterious brewing process and went over to the filing cabinets.

"Refiling *again*?" he asked.

She nodded. "Reverse numeric, by application number; first preliminaries, then finals."

He frowned at the office door.

"She's toying with you."

Violet did not disagree.

When it was ready, Ben poured himself a cup. Violet always kept a clean cup for him on the bottom shelf.

"Odds are, the kid's going to be fine. You know how good the docs are. They see this kind of thing all the time."

"Every one hundred seventy-three days, give or take," she said. He couldn't see her face: she was bowed over the filing cabinet.

"Say, you get a chance, I was thinking we might look into that whale thing. Like, what are the chances the whales might be looking for something like an improved blowhole? Otherwise it's hard to figure why Doctor Petaja would be so interested."

She paused, still bent over the drawers. "I think the League of Robotic Persons has been in communication with the whales. It was in the newsletter."

This was news to Ben, but then he wasn't on their mailing list. "Maybe you could look into that?"

"You're trying to work me, Ben."

He sipped his coffee. "Well, of course I am. It's not like you wouldn't do the same."

He got up and walked over to the wastebasket. "Hey, look what I found," he told her. "Looks like these fell off your desk, right into the trash."

Violet closed a file drawer and looked at the applications. "Oh, it looks like they want to be investigators," she said.

"Who wouldn't? We get all those swell benefits."

He picked them up, flipped through them, and dropped them back into the wastebasket. "But we've got real qualified people who are first in line. It's a fact. And that kid's going to be fine, you know. Those scientists! Always on the lookout for an experimental subject. *They* have a lot to answer for."

Violet went back to the filing drawer that had recently been marked 'M', but now read '1311.569 - 1220.482'.

"Whales, was it?" she asked.

"Yeah, whales, as in, what are they after, and how would they pay for it, and should we be worried?"

"We should always be worried," Violet said. "That's our job."

Ben poured himself a second cup. "Yep. That's us. We worry."

He didn't mention it, but he was going to check on things in the Infirmary before he went home.

Next morning Ben stopped by the Infirmary again to visit with Officer Binder. The frog's legs were bigger now – a *lot* bigger – and the hair on the back of the kid's head was thinning and falling out to reveal a glossy green, yellow-spotted scalp.

The kid was taking it well. His eyes looked like they'd grown a bit larger, too, but it was hard to be sure because they were tending toward the wide and terrified.

The nurse was smiling in a fixed, manic way that wasn't very reassuring. "Officer Binder is such a *good* patient," she said.

"You just get some rest and heal up," Ben told him. "We're really short-handed out there, you know. Everybody's looking forward to getting you back."

Officer Binder thanked him for dropping by.

Ben realized that he was staring at those frog's legs. Every few seconds they'd give a little kick. He had to force himself to look away, 'cause it was kind of interesting.

"No more of those macaroons, right?" he called on his way out. The kid bobbed his head and flicked his long, purple tongue from side to side.

Ben found that Violet wasn't at her desk, but she had a fresh pot of coffee bubbling on the sideboard. He helped himself and was settling into the guest chair when she came out of the Registrar's office. "You have a message," she told him, and she dug out a little yellow slip next to her typewriter.

It was from Doctor Petaja. He had a new batch of preliminary applications and several final applications to file. Ben's shoulders sank.

"I was hoping I'd have more time," he admitted.

"I have a call in to Hazel at the League of Robotic Persons. About your whales."

"Yeah, okay. Well, it'll be interesting to see which of his preliminaries made it to final, I guess. Might tell us something."

"You see the new kid?"

"Yeah, he's looking swell. Gonna just shrug it off, I think."

They sat for a bit in a companionable silence.

"That filing business settle down?"

Violet turned to face the files. "It's still early."

Ben finished his coffee, rinsed the cup, and told Violet he'd see her later. He was just going to have to face Doctor Petaja and collect the new paperwork. No sense in putting it off.

Things were pretty lively in the District that morning; something to do with rogue emanations from a ray at Doctor Price's place. Big lead shields were standing in the streets all around the laboratory. Somebody with an Info-Slate kept calling out new positions for them, and each time he did a squad of lab assistants would run out, roll the shields into a new position, and then fall back to the alleys. Everyone looked tense.

So Doctor Petaja's parlor, with its ring of motionless robots, almost felt like a sanctuary.

The doctor was in a strange state. He'd jump up, fiddle with something or other, and freeze for a moment with his head twitching to the left; then he'd settle down, jump up, and start the cycle over again. It looked to Ben as though he was starting to show the effects of the Essential Neural Energizer. It made for an odd sort of conversation.

As the doctor froze again, Ben paged through the final applications. There were forty new preliminaries – fewer than he'd feared – but the finals were the thing he was most interested in. He saw that *Enhanced Method of Air Expulsion for Cetaceans, Proposed Technique for Liquefying Cellular Material By Means Of Distant Modified Rainfall,* and *Completely Revised Application of Highly Energized Light Rays in the Analysis of Atmospheric Composition* had all been completed. He barely glanced at the new preliminaries; it would take days to assess whether they were a threat.

The doctor continued his abandoned sentence as though he hadn't just broken off to twitch for the past minute and a half. "...and I hope there won't be any delays in processing the final applications, Investigator. I see great potential in all of them."

"Well, you know we need to look for issues of prior art, Doctor. To make sure you aren't infringing on any other inventor's patents. That can take some time, even when we're not struggling along with a skeleton staff. I don't think we can accelerate – "

Ben stopped. Doctor Petaja had just jumped straight into the air and fallen to the floor.

The twelve formerly motionless robots creaked into action: two of them stepped to the doctor while the others scattered throughout the laboratory. Carrying the unconscious doctor to a niche in the wall, his two guardians pulled

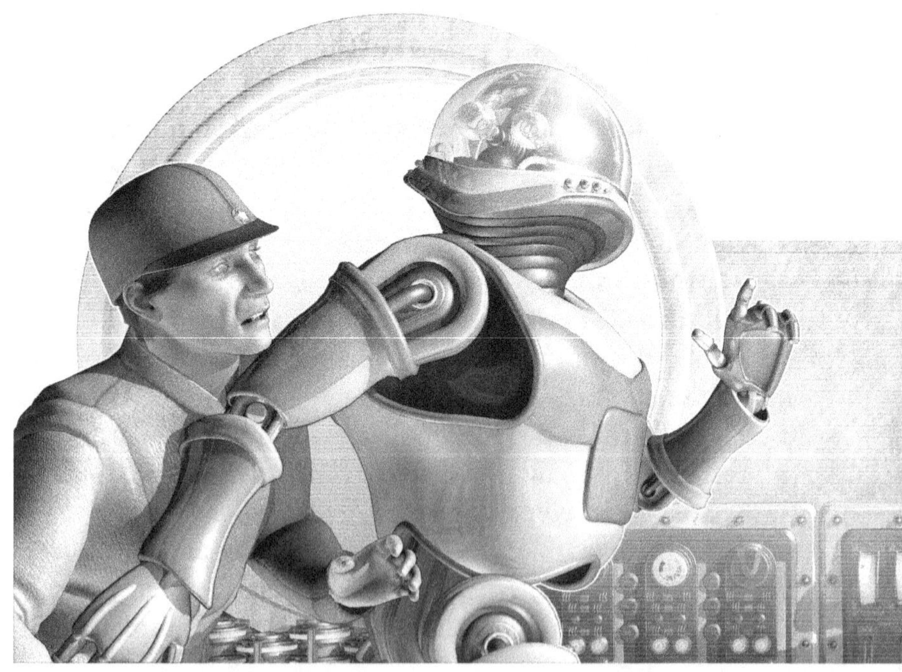

on a hidden lever. The niche disgorged a metallic capsule, about the size of a sarcophagus, that was closed with thick steel straps. A third robot unlocked the straps and opened the capsule. Doctor Petaja was lowered, quite carefully, inside. The three robots carried the capsule out of the parlor and down the hall.

Eight more robots were working their way through the laboratory. Ben could hear heavy shutters falling into place; the laboratory's exterior doors were sealed with blast gates, and in every way the laboratory was being secured around him.

The twelfth robot came to rest in front of Ben.

"Doctor Petaja regrets that he has been temporarily incapacitated," it said in its huge voice. "We will seal the front door behind you. If you have any pending business with the doctor, he should be available again in approximately one hundred and twenty days. Thank you for your speedy cooperation in this matter."

Then the robot picked Ben up and carried him out to the front steps. Doctor Petaja's door crashed closed, and Ben heard a blast door roll into place behind it.

"Well," he said aloud. "That's something."

Apparently he now had another one hundred and twenty days to figure out what the doctor had been up to. The Essential Neural Energizer, despite its ridiculous enhancements to productivity, wasn't a completely bad thing.

Ben started to whistle on his way back to the office.

Ben was surprised by some of Violet's news from the League of Robotic Persons. But as an experienced investigator he knew how to nod, one eyebrow lowered, as though she was just confirming what he'd suspected all along.

"They sure can hold a grudge," he said.

The Registrar also lowered one eyebrow when Ben brought Violet with him into their meeting.

Ben delivered the news that Doctor Petaja was out of the picture for the next four months. That would give them all time to deal with this although, by its nature, it was now a matter for City Government. He gave an overview of the preliminary applications and their finals; he expressed the clear concerns raised by the applications; and then he turned it over to Violet, saying "But it was Violet who cracked this thing, ma'am. Her tireless research and her, uh, penetrating insights, I mean. They were the thing that turned the corner."

The Registrar turned to Violet. "Explain."

"In the long run, Registrar, it was the involvement of the whales and the combination of the technologies that made things clear. The League of Robotic Persons has set up a dialogue with the world's cetaceans, who have a name for their organization that I can't pronounce. It means something like 'Seawide Alliance of Thoughtful Persons'. They've found that humans are very interested in some materials that can be found on the sea floor. Some very *valuable* materials, easily retrieved by the whales. And although no one has really noticed, the whales now have large accounts with several of the city's banking institutions."

"Are they using shell companies, holding companies, that sort of thing?"

"No, Registrar. They've been conducting their business right out in the open. It's just that it never occurred to anyone that – "

"Yes, I see. Go on."

Ben interrupted. "I was really impressed with Violet's reasoning, here," he said. "She's showing a natural aptitude for – "

"That's enough, Investigator. Violet?"

The robot secretary ground her steely foot into Ben's instep. He kept smiling, somehow, while she continued.

"It turns out that there's a radical group within the Seawide Alliance of Thoughtful Persons.This group has bitter memories of the days when human people *hunted* whales, ma'am. They're not convinced that, beg your pardon, you've changed your ways on a permanent basis. And so they feel that the whales should have some means of self defense."

The Registrar scratched a note on her notepad. "This is starting to sound like a diplomatic problem," she said.

"Very likely, ma'am. It turns out that Doctor Petaja received a research commission from the Seawide Alliance. Several of these new patents are the result of his research."

Ben spread the final applications across the Registrar's spotless desk. He pointed at each one.

"If I may? First we have the *Completely Revised Application of Highly Energized Light Rays in the Analysis of Atmospheric Composition.* That's useful in, say, atmospheric analysis for weather prediction, or in detecting pollutants. Also, as we'll see here, it has applications in targeting and range finding. Next there's *Proposed Technique for Liquefying Cellular Material By Means Of Distant Modified Rainfall* which, of course, sounds kind of alarming to anybody who's made of cellular material, like, heh heh, you or me. But the 'rainfall' thing seems strange, until you combine it with *Enhanced Method of Air Expulsion for Cetaceans.* Because when they breathe out, those whales are expelling a heck of a lot of water vapor. So when you put all of these together – " he put the three applications into a single stack. " – what you get is a sophisticated range-finding system, combined with a disintegrating mist that's delivered through the use of modified blowholes for the whales. With, uh, a range of about seventy miles."

He straightened. "It's probably meant to protect the whales from any kind of whaling operation," he said. "Though once they have the technology...."

The Registrar looked solemn. "Yes, they might just decide to use it."

"But ma'am, did I mention that it was Violet who put all of this together?"

"Yes, Investigator. I think you may have mentioned it."

The Registrar looked at Violet. "I'll need to call a meeting with representatives from City Government," she said. "Also, because they seem to be so helpful, with the League of Robotic Persons."

Violet started for the door, but turned. "It's worth noting that *Proposed Technique for Liquefying Cellular Material* has some superficial resemblance to Professor Zappencackler's Patent #13,559. We could tie that up in an investigation for several months. Actually, indefinitely. If that's a help."

As the door swung shut Ben smiled helpfully. "She's just done this amazing job here," he said.

The Registrar smiled back. "Yes, she really has. On your way out, could you tell Violet that I've had a fascinating new idea about the filing system? I'd like her to get right on it."

Ben forgot to leave, until she reminded him.

Violet was still refiling, two days later, when Registrar Finlay went up to City Hall for the Whales Meeting.

Ben was pretty riled up about it. But Violet took the long view. "She's a worthy opponent," was all she'd say.

One of the mail room boys came in with a package.

"For the Registrar?" Violet asked.

"No, ma'am, this one's for you." He set the package on her desk, and she rose from the file drawers to look at it.

"For me?"

The boy asserted that this was true. Then, to Ben: "So we saw Officer Binder off this morning. Early retirement, full pension."

Ben was pleased to hear it. "And did they ever get it off?"

"No, sorry to say. The docs called it 'inoperable'. Fact is, they're not even sure his own head is still in there."

They all took a moment to imagine what it would be like to have a giant bullfrog for a head.

"He was – I mean, he's a nice kid," Ben said at last.

"Yeah, he was always real popular down in the mail room."

They all thought about it some more.

"Full pension, though?" Ben asked.

"Yeah, no problems there. Everybody was real nice about it, too."

The boy from the mail room continued on his rounds. Violet unwrapped her package and she sank into her chair, lifting the little trophy from its bed of wrapping paper.

"Hey! Employee of the Month!" Ben was beaming. "Congratulations!"

Violet looked up from the trophy. "This isn't over," she said.

VOLTO VAC
EMPLOYE
OF THE MONT
MARCH

WHERE TO GO? HOW TO GET THERE? WHAT TO DO ONCE YOU ARRIVE?

These questions, so vexing to new arrivals, are our stock in trade at the Retropolis Travel Bureau.

Anywhere in the city you can visit us at our many convenient offices and we'll be happy to answer them.

But wouldn't it be better if those answers were right in your pocket?

That's why we've prepared this useful guidebook. It's available, at reasonable cost, at all our offices.

Learn how the city's public transportation system can speed you from one landmark to another! You'll whisk yourself and your family from the Perisquare straight to the Pi Monument in spacious Circle Square, and you'll do it with all the confidence of a native Retropolitan.

AVAILABLE AT RETROPOLIS TRAVEL BUREAU OFFICES CITYWIDE - VISIT US AT THE MAIN MONORAIL TERMINAL

SPONSORED BY RAY-O-ZAP

THIS IS A SERIOUS SPORTING EVENT
NOISY DEMONSTRATIONS WILL
NOT BE TOLERATED

SERVING THE HOME & TRADE

ROSIE'S GARAGE

ROCKET ENGINES - SPARE PARTS
CUSTOM MACHINERY - SALVAGE
ALL BOUGHT AND SOLD

Mysteries resolved. Questions answered. Perplexing puzzles explained. All at reasonable rates.

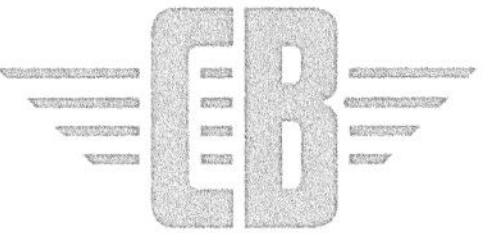

You know where to find him.
We know you do.

Fenwick's Improved Venomous Worms

With

Ben Bowman

and

Violet

From the files of the Retropolis Registry of Patents

Violet wasn't at her desk, so Ben helped himself to some of her coffee – so much better than the usual office pot – and found himself looking at the three 'Employee of the Month' trophies that were arranged in a row on one of the file cabinets.

He'd seen them before, of course. But just now he realized that they weren't quite normal.

You'd expect something like a winged Victory, or an athlete, or (if budgets were tight) maybe a recycled bowler. These trophies looked more like Atlas, bearing the weight of the world on his shoulders. But this fella's shoulders didn't seem quite wide enough for the job. You couldn't help but notice, when you looked really closely, that he was bent over and straining with everything he had; and there was this feeling that he wasn't going to be able to keep it up much longer. He looked like he ought to be trembling under the weight. Ben bent over to look into the face of one of the trophies just as Violet came back through the Registrar's door with a stack of papers in her enameled, metallic arms.

He nodded at her and pointed to the trophy's face. "His face," Ben said. "The expression. It looks...."

"It's agony," the robot secretary told him.

He took a step back. "Yeah, my thought. That's... well, that's unusual, isn't it?"

"It's a custom design," Violet said. She sat down behind her desk. "Registrar Finlay designed them herself."

Ben took a sip of Violet's excellent coffee. He looked again at the row of trophies.

"And, so far, she's only given them to you...?"

"That's right," Violet told him. "Just me."

"Well, three months running."

"Yes. I'd say she has a particular regard for my job performance."

Ben eased over to the desk, where he could get a look at that stack of papers Violet was sorting.

"Hey, that's a lot of invitations!"

Each of the papers seemed to be a notification that Registrar Finlay had received an award and was expected to speak; or an invitation to a conference, where it was hoped that she might speak; or an inquiry about her availability on the night of a banquet, convention, or fundraiser, where – if it wasn't any trouble – she might consider delivering a speech...?

"Oh, yes. The Registrar's very much in demand at the moment. So many speeches. She can't possibly make it to all of them. In fact, she was looking for you, just now."

Ben bought himself a moment by pouring a fresh cup of coffee. There was an intense battle of wills in progress between the Registrar and her secretary. Ben would always take Violet's side, of course: partly because they were friends, and partly because he knew what happened to anybody who was on the *other* side. But he was doing his best to stay out of the crossfire.

"Looking for me?"

"Yes. I think she had some kind of assignment for you." Violet's head rose for a moment. She looked at him with what might have been concern, though you couldn't really tell. "You might not like it much."

So Ben was working out how he could disappear for the day when the Registrar herself came through her office door. "Investigator Bowman. I was hoping I might find you."

There wasn't any way to avoid her now. Ben followed her through into her office, where she closed the door behind him and took a seat. She waved at the guest chair. "Please, sit."

He sank into the chair and worked up a smile. When the

Registrar didn't smile back his eyes wandered to the bookshelf behind her: it was piled with trophies, awards, and plaques. "Say," he tried, "it looks like you've got quite a collection there, ma'am."

Registrar Finlay shifted in her chair. She didn't look at her trove of awards. "Yes. I think someone may have been recommending me for those, and for a lot of public speaking. I don't suppose you know anything about that?"

Ben shook his head.

"In fact," the Registrar went on, "I seem to have two speeches to make today. So I'd like you to make one of them for me."

Ben continued to shake his head, now much more quickly. "Oh, no, I don't think.... That is, I'm not really... you wouldn't want me to...uh. I'm not very...."

"You'll do fine, Investigator. I think this lecture will be something you're *uniquely qualified* for. You just need to make a speech about the Registry of Patents, over at the Retropolis Academy for the Unusually Inventive."

Ben stuttered into a terrified silence.

"Your *alma mater*, I believe."

The years Ben had spent at the Academy were, he had hoped, well behind him – except in nightmares. Oh, he had some *amazing* nightmares.

The Retropolis Academy for the Unusually Inventive is the only place in the city where students can study science. Oh, there are plenty of engineering schools, plenty of general universities, and many, many schools for younger students. But any students in those other schools who start to show the telltale signs of a *scientific* mind are swiftly transferred to the Academy. They might escape notice when they memorize the Periodic Table; they can easily slip by if they tinker with the chemicals in a chemistry lab; but the moment they build their first Antimatter Catapult or High Energy Squirrel Emulsifier, their teachers pull them out of class and pack them off to the one school that's prepared to deal with their particular talents. Once they arrive they're on a fast track program that will one day release them into the Experimental Research District – the only place in Retropolis, by statute, where scientific research can be pursued.

Having entered the Academy there was, normally, only the one outcome: a lifelong career in the middle of the explosions and the sometimes successful transmogrifications that punctuate both the District and quite a few of the careers we just mentioned, with punctuation marks like the period, the exclamation mark, and, now and then, the question mark. In careers of this type, an ellipsis is extremely rare.

In a few cases a student might wash out of the Academy and return to a normal life.

Ben had very badly wanted a normal life.

"I really think, ma'am, I mean, I'm sure that one of the other investigators would...."

"I'm sorry, Investigator Bowman. I'm afraid my mind's quite made up. They expect you at one o'clock."

"Or Violet! Violet's memorized all the files, she's a great... she'd give a terrific lecture, Registrar. She'd be...."

The Registrar gave Ben a cool, thoughtful look.

"Maybe you'd like to take Violet with you, then, as a resource. But you must deliver the lecture yourself." She finally turned to look at her stack of awards and certificates. "Violet may have had too much free time on her hands, lately."

"I'm so sorry, Ben," Violet said. "I double booked her. I didn't mean to."

"The tests, the hazing, the... the *exercises*...."

"And it never occurred to me that she'd drag you into this. I've just been trying..."

"They put things in your *locker*. Things that leap out and attach themselves to your *face*..."

"...to keep her out of the office, and to give her a very high profile..."

"...with *suckers*. And, and *tentacles*. And they *talk* to you..."

"...so that some other agency would notice how popular she is..."

"...and the *lunches*! I still have these dreams about the *lunches*!"

Ben and Violet came out of the monorail terminal near the Academy. They could see it, three blocks down, its façade a massive, pilastered, windowless block. An heroic statue of Thales of Miletus loomed over the Academy's open doors. Unlike Violet's trophies,Thales didn't look as though he was about to be crushed by the weight of the world.

"It's *hard* to flunk out of the Academy! You have to do it in these slight, subtle stages..."

"You know she'll never make me an investigator, Ben. Just like the other Registrars. So, as always, I just need to..."

"...like, in every test I just did *slightly* worse. One by one. Quarter by quarter. Until finally my tests were just so bad they had to think I wasn't equipped for science at the higher levels. Like, I was just a *little* gifted. But I had to do it slowly. It took *years*."

Violet took him by the arm. "I know, Ben. You *majored* in washing out."

At that moment, when at last they were having the same conversation, both of them fell silent.

"We need to be there in fifteen minutes," Violet said at last.

"I never thought I'd have to go back."

She led him down the street. "I'll be with you," she told him. "You just need to give the lecture, and then we'll get out immediately. I promise."

They came to the Academy's entryway, with that huge façade hanging over them. "She knew exactly what she was doing," Violet said. "She won't get away with this. I've been working on that."

Ben wasn't listening.

The Academy's atrium was fifteen stories tall. Galleries ringed it, one above another, until the walls met high overhead in a domed skylight. All along the galleries the students rushed from one classroom to another. There were collisions, some of them violent, between the young scientists and their projects. Their voices and detonations echoed all through the entry space, in whose center two huge glass cylinders rose fifty feet above the floor. In each one was a thirty-foot worm.

"*Eunice aphroditois*?" Violet wondered. "But they're normally aquatic. And, of course, not so large."

"Oh, yes," said a voice behind her. "Magnificent, aren't they? Spines loaded with neurotoxins, and those *extremely* powerful jaws.They can digest almost anything. Beautiful creatures."

Violet turned; Ben jumped. It turned out to be Professor Zappencackler. "That's the senior project of one of our most promising students. Young Fenwick. He'll be in your audience, of course. So nice to see you, Ben! And Miss Violet."

"They're pretty big worms, normally," Violet said. "But these are exceptional. And... land dwelling, apparently?"

"Oh, my, yes. You certainly wouldn't want to run into *these* babies out on the street."

Ben finally found his voice. "And, uh, what are you going to do with them...?"

That stopped Professor Zappencackler short. "*Do* with them? Oh, I have no idea. But that's your Patent Investigator talking, there. These things don't have to serve a *purpose*. They just have to be...."

"...interesting," Ben finished.

"Yes! That's exactly it!" the Professor grinned. "And they certainly are."

The three of them stared at the gigantic, carnivorous, venomous worms with several degrees of interest. The worms, their segmented and colorful bodies writhing, were mainly concerned with escape.

"But we're almost late for your lecture," the Professor said. "We must get to the auditorium!"

The auditorium doors stood directly opposite the Academy's entrance, but as the speaker Ben had to be led through a narrow hall alongside the large room, around to the back of the stage, and finally to the wings. Violet stayed close behind him.

Ben swayed slightly as he stood behind the curtain. "But why are there *two* of the worms?" he asked, though he was pretty sure of the answer.

"For breeding, of course!"

Professor Zappencackler left them, approaching the lectern to the sound of faint, scattered applause.

"Because you can't have enough giant flesh-eating venomous worms," Violet concluded.

Ben nodded. "I really hate this place."

"Today's lecture should be of great interest to all of you," said Professor Zappencackler. "We're fortunate to have an investigator from the Registry of Patents, who will explain how the Registry determines which inventions are unique, and which inventors will receive the royalties from those inventions that have commercial applications."

There was a sound like waves washing out along a shoreline. The students had slumped in their seats and, in the back of the auditorium, had started up a few quiet conversations.

"But as interesting as *that* is," the Professor went on, "you'll be thrilled to know more about our guest lecturer, Ben Bowman. Investigator Bowman is a legend among the Academy faculty. We remember him well! Over the course of four years, Investigator Bowman became the *single worst student* ever to walk the Academy halls. There wasn't a single subject his brain could contain! His decline was so remarkable that it's now the centerpiece of Professor Maepenn's paper on *Rapid Cognitive Decline Expressed Through Graphs and Measurements*. Having the famously deficient Investigator Bowman here is a genuine treat that I'm sure you will enjoy. Investigator?"

The Professor was smiling and waving at Ben, who stood motionless behind the curtain.

"Just use lots of statistics," Violet said. She was shoving him forward. "Statistics will be your friend, here."

Ben lurched out onto the stage. The audience leaned forward to get a closer look at the Academy's most complete failure; then two-thirds of them sank back. There was that chance that his condition might be contagious. Ben managed a fragile smile.

Zappencackler tapped him on the shoulder as he stepped to the podium.

"Make the old *alma mater* proud, boy!"

Ben's one consolation was that – unlike in the dreams – he was pretty sure he still had his pants on. He looked down. Oh, yes. Pants. He gazed out over the silent crowd. Somebody in the far rows coughed.

Ben decided to start with a joke.

"...and so then the mathematician – no, sorry, I mean the logician. It was the mathematician who said that last bit. The one, you know, that... anyway, then the logician says, *in fact what we see is that one sheep in Scotland is black... on one side*."

He waited for the laughter. The crowd, though, was just sort of staring at him with the kind of fascination you get when something unexpected and disturbing shows up under the microscope, without its pants on.

Ben swallowed. From the wings, Violet was hissing at him: "*Use statistics!*"

"Uh, thirty-two per cent of you thought that was funny, but don't want to say so," he tried. He shot Violet a smile. *That's statistical*, he thought. *That's what you call a statistic.*

From there he launched into a brief history of the Registry of Patents, its charter, and what everyone thought its function was, because you never mention in public that the Registry is a form of oversight over the scientists in the Experimental Research District. He could see that he was losing his grip on – at least – the audience; so he went on to describe very successful inventions and the fortunes they'd made for the scientists who created them. He was on slightly firmer ground there, he could see. The *Energetic Earth-Displacing Behemoth* (Patent #14,529) was always a crowd pleaser. So he went on with the *Previously Unsuspected Method for Gravity Inversion* (Patent #12,449) and the *All-Encompassing Mood Sensing Toroidal System in a Compact Device* (Patent #8,922). But those weren't so compelling to the audience, maybe because they had so little potential for destruction. So Ben's brow bunched up into a knot of wrinkles as he tried to think of some Registry statistics.

"But, uh, those commercial applications can't be the only focus of your research," he tried. "Because, uh, what you must always do is to... uh, to forge forward through the boundaries of human knowledge." The students looked as though they liked that one. "Royalties, though not very interesting in themselves, provide you with the wealth you need to expand your laboratory. To purchase expensive equipment and materials, uh, of a kind that your neighbors can't afford. To, uh, become a towering giant of scientific innovation before whom, uh, who – no, whom! – all other scientists must, well, *bow in deference*. Royalties are the fuel that drives you to... to *utter domination* in the Experimental Research District."

The students hesitated, then started to applaud in little groups.

Ben couldn't believe it: he had them. He drew in a breath, while Violet signaled frantically from the wings, and prepared to sink the hook into his audience. "With *substantial* royalties, you can rise above the – "

The doors at the far end of the auditorium flew open. Four students rushed in and cried, *"Mole people!"*

Ben stopped for a moment. "No, you don't get mole people in June. What I meant was – "

But by then he could see that something was going wrong out in the atrium. Tiny, suited figures were headed toward the auditorium doors. Some kind of gigantic drilling machine had thrust up through the tiles. A horde of mole people was spilling out from the machine's cabin.

"Uh, we ought to do something about those doors," he said. But it was too late: the mole people had slammed them shut.

"They have welding gear!" one of the students shouted. The crack between the doors was already heating to a dull red. From the rear rows of the auditorium a group of students jumped up to shove the doors open, but it was already too late. They were trapped inside.

"Huh," Ben said. "Really, you just don't get mole people this early in the summer." Nobody was listening any more, so he edged back into the stage's wings.

Professor Zappencackler and Violet were whispering back and forth.

"In June!" Ben said. "Can you believe it?"

Professor Zappencackler shushed him. "They've blocked the main doors, but they probably missed the hallway," he said. "Hurry!"

So the three of them hurried down the narrow corridor alongside the auditorium. When they reached the door, they cracked it open and looked out into the atrium.

The mole people had assembled in front of the two glass tubes that housed the immense *Eunice aphroditois* specimens. The tubes seemed to worry them: one mole person was rapping the nearest tube with a mallet. They were all carrying long crooks and ray guns. The crooks, Ben supposed, were meant for worm wrangling. But it looked like they hadn't ex-

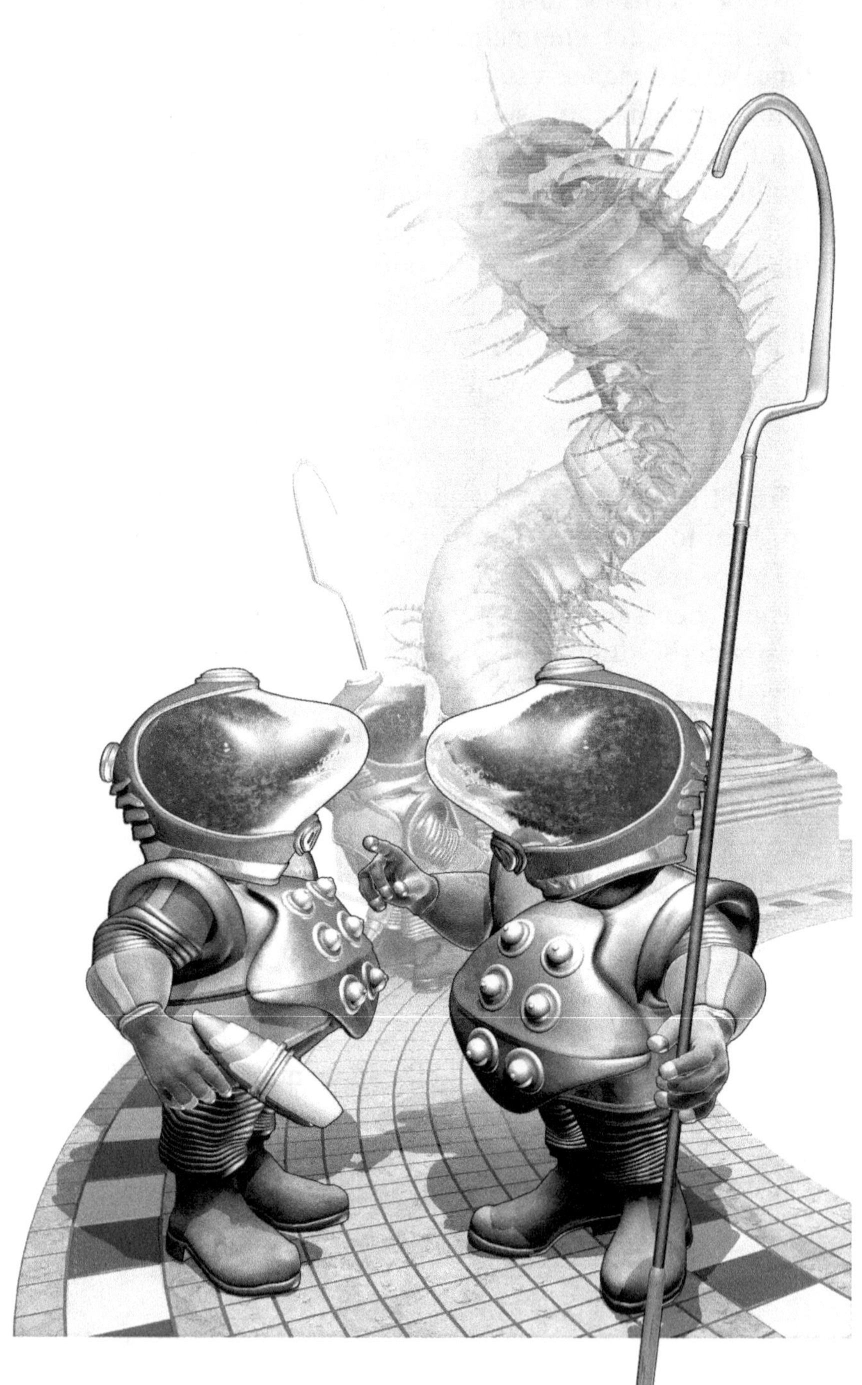

pected the great glassy containers.

"Do you suppose those fellas came for the worms?" Ben asked.

"They're not fellows," the Professor corrected him. "Just look at the, um, the chest area."

Each mole person's chest armor was studded with six tiny breast cups.

"The males invariably fight when they meet," Violet said. "So if you run into a group of mole people, they're always female."

The mole persons, each about three feet in height, gathered in a ring in front of the worm tubes. Some kind of discussion seemed to be going on.

"We should get young Fenwick," said the Professor. "And whatever useful devices the students are carrying." So Ben ran back through the hallway to call for volunteers.

Fenwick was, indeed, young: obviously a prodigy. The devices were more or less useful; mainly less, to be honest. But the Spherical Obfuscator could be of use, and even the Hand-Held Universal Moisture Remover might come in handy. Ben guided his charges back to the doorway. The Professor and Violet had by then decided what was going on and were working on a plan for getting the mole people back underground, where they belonged.

"But you can't *talk* to them," the Professor snapped. "They're *moles*."

"But, what they're wearing... and the drilling machine...."

"Still moles. Oh, they communicate in some way, but we've never worked out how."

Violet poked her enameled head through the door. "They're... they're snuffling," she said.

It was true: the mole helmets had a kind of grating at the front, and it looked like the moles could sniff odors through them.

"Very sensitive to odors, your mole." Professor Zappencackler looked back at Ben's students. "Fenwick! What can you tell me about this?"

The young genius shuffled to the front and peered through the door. "I think they smelled my worms," he said.

Zappencackler slapped the boy's head. "Of course they smelled your worms! But how?"

"It may have been the way I added the neurotoxins," Fenwick told him. He didn't seem to mind the slap, but of course he'd be used to that by now. "*Eunice aphroditois* isn't venomous by nature."

"Really?" Violet asked. "But I thought they were."

"No. That's a myth," Fenwick said. "Until now, I mean. I made that little improvement."

The group of them turned to look out at Fenwick's thirty-foot long improved venomous worms. The worms had grown still, their brightly colored heads turned toward the mole people.

"I wonder if the mole people know," said Ben.

"What about insects?" Ben asked. "Don't moles eat insects too?"

Professor Zappencackler waved him off. "If they'd rather have insects, why come *here*? Either worms are a delicacy to them, or the sheer size of Fenwick's worms means that they can feed their city for months; maybe years, if they breed the things."

The mole people had run their drilling machine clear out of the floor. Its huge drill was aimed at one of the worm enclosures.

"I didn't know I'd made them smell *good*," Fenwick was saying. "Who knows what smells good to a mole person?"

Violet patted him on the back. "Well, I guess we know now," she said. "You've managed to create a mole attractor of unprecedented power."

"Yes... I have, haven't I?" The boy's face brightened.

"Now we just have to figure out how to make a mole repellent that's even *more* effective."

This was the problem, all right. Ben was making an inventory of the devices the students were carrying. "We could try something with odors," he suggested. "Some smell that the moles just can't stand. I think their helmets might even be concentrating the odors around them, like loudspeakers."

"That would explain the suits and helmets," Professor Zappencackler said. "Isolation from most odors, concentration of the most vital. It probably has something to do with the way they're communicating."

"So a powerful smell might repel them and prevent them from talking to each other...." Ben handed back the Encapsulated Note-Taking Recording and Retrieval System. "Don't let them catch you with that during the exams," he advised. The young woman who'd been carrying it slipped it back into her pocket and looked sidelong at the Professor.

"It sounds like *you* could have used one of these," she whispered.

Ben chose to ignore that.

"But it all goes sideways if the worms get out," said Fenwick. "I could make a break for it, run upstairs, get my Worm Handler Suit. It's impervious to their venomous spines."

But a look out at the crowd of mole people showed that this would be a suicide mission. Even the students in the upstairs galleries had drawn back from the railings after a few well-placed shots from the moles' ray guns. Someone was whimpering in the gallery directly above.

"At the very least," said the Professor, "we need to stop them from using their drilling machine on the tubes. Maybe if they can't get at the worms they'll just give up and go away."

Three of the students were removing the hinges from the hallway door. That ought to keep the mole people from sealing them in. It would also leave the hall exposed to fire from their ray guns, Ben thought.

"Say," he said, "what's the range on that Spherical Obfuscator?"

One of the students handed it to him. "You can get three or four people in there," she said. "Maybe six, if they're not claustrophobic." She was looking at Ben as though she figured he was really, *really* claustrophobic.

"*Six*, then," he said with a grim smile. "Six of us can sneak up on the drilling machine and take it over, if we're concealed by the Obfuscator. We just close the hatch behind us, and they're stuck outside."

Everyone looked at him. "You know," Fenwick whispered, "he really doesn't *seem* that... backward."

Violet slapped the side of Fenwick's head that Zappencackler hadn't slapped earlier. "Show some respect, young man."

Since a slap from Violet's steel hand wasn't anything to joke about, young Fenwick showed something that looked like respect. Pained respect, maybe, but Ben had to take it where he could find it around here.

"So me, and Violet, and the Professor, and maybe Fenwick – in case his worms get loose – and a couple of you...?"

Only one – the young woman who'd brought the Spherical Obfuscator – volunteered.

"Five might do it," Ben allowed.

With its hinges removed, the three students at the door were holding it in place so the mole people couldn't see them. The five members of the Mole Persons Repellent Squad gathered together in a tight squeeze. The Spherical Obfuscator whined into life, and they were surrounded by a globe that projected whatever was visible from the back side of the sphere, as you faced it, onto the front. They were now effectively invisible. "Let the door go now," Ben whispered, and it swept out of their way. There was a minor problem when it swept back, just a little too soon, but Fenwick contained his

grunt and then they were out on the atrium floor.

From the inside, the Sphere was a little confusing. In front of them they could see a perfect image of what was actually behind them, and it was only behind them that they could see where they were going. So the group of five pivoted in place inside their concealing globe and walked backwards, sneaking up on the drilling machine. Its motor was chugging softly while the mole people approached the right-hand tube with their worm crooks extended.

The Mole Persons Repellent Squad crept under the shadow of the drilling machine and positioned themselves below its open hatch. There was no way they'd be able to get through the hatch while walking backwards, so they waited until the mole people had reached the tube before they switched off the device and leaped, one by one, into the cabin.

This exposed the flaw in Ben's plan. A crew of four mole people in their bronze and leather suits were hunched over the machine's controls. Although they seemed quite surprised to see a party of five join them, they pulled ray guns from their holsters and neatly surrounded Ben and his companions. One, who seemed to be their leader, made a couple of emphatic *meeps*.

Ben raised his hands over his head. "We come in peace, ladies," he said. Then, more quietly, he added "Everybody try not to smell like a worm."

Without the mole people's tiny, agile hands at the controls the drilling machine's motor ascended into a dangerous whine. They all stumbled as it lurched forward, its rotating blade driving straight at the right-hand worm tube. Inside the tube, the worm recoiled; the mole people that faced it stepped back in dismay.

Poor Fenwick had been in the rear, so when the drilling machine struck the heavy glass worm enclosure he was thrown right out of the hatch and onto the atrium floor.

He's having a rotten day, Ben thought. But the mole people in the cabin had also been thrown around. Three had lost their ray guns. Ben snatched the last of the ray guns from the mole leader and trained it on her. That out of the way, he was able to do what everyone else was doing: he stared through the windshield at what had recently been an impregnable glass worm container. Now the thirty-foot worm was slinking out between the shards of broken glass. Its venomous spines were twitching.

"Okay," Ben said. "We need a new plan."

The worm reached the nearest of the mole women. Its spiky head shot down and pierced the leather of her suit. In an instant her back arched and she fell to the floor, writhing briefly, before her helmeted body grew stiff in front of their eyes.

"You see that?" Ben asked the mole leader. He waved the ray gun at the worm. "They're *poisonous*. You can't tame 'em. Heck, you probably can't even *eat* 'em."

The little mole woman couldn't understand the words, but it looked like she was getting the idea. She leaned forward and *meeped* into a microphone. But the moles didn't fall back. They held their worm crooks out straight in front of them and tried to surround the worm.

Fenwick, alone in the shadow of the drilling machine, rose from the floor and tried to reason with the mole people. He didn't have any more luck than Ben.

"Fenwick!" Violet shouted. "Behind you! The worm!"

Young Fenwick tried to dive for the underside of the drilling machine, but too late. His body rose, squirming and jerking, clasped in the mouth parts of his Improved Worm. The venomous spines had already got him.

"Oh, *Fenwick*," breathed the young woman with the Spherical Obfuscator.

"He's already gone," Violet said. She tapped Ben's shoulder on her way through the hatch.

"Wait!" Professor Zappencackler called. He threw the Hand-Held Universal Moisture Remover after her, and she caught it without slowing on her way toward the venomous worm.

Ben was miming eating in front of the mole leader. Then he clutched his head and writhed on the floor. "Poisonous! Get it?" She ignored him as she *meeped* more orders into the microphone.

“She must think they can eat the worms anyway,” the Sphere bearer said. “Maybe they can. But how can they catch them?”

The mole people were forming into a double line. The front line kept their crooks extended, while the back line aimed their ray guns at the worm. It had dropped Fenwick’s body and was now looking at the second glassy worm tube, from which its comrade was observing events with interest. The great worm inched toward the unbroken tube and began to coil around it.

Violet leaped onto its tail, the Hand-Held Universal Moisture Remover in one hand, and she began to scale its spiny back. The worm reflexively struck at her with its spines. This had no effect on a robot, of course, but the worm kept trying anyway. Violet ran lightly up its back and wrapped her legs around what we will – for convenience – call its neck, brandishing the Hand-Held Universal Moisture Remover. She fired off a blast.

The Hand-Held Universal Moisture Remover emitted a small but devastating cone of dessication: three spines on the worm’s face crumbled away into dust. The worm came to an immediate stop; it seemed be be considering the situation. Its tail lashed up at Violet, but she held on and the tail spines snapped off when they tried to puncture her metallic body. The worm slowly loosened its grip on the tube and it slithered onto the floor, only to face the ranks of mole persons. Their little faces were set in expressions of grim intent, and they advanced in step. Violet twisted upright on the worm’s neck.

The worm crooks looked useless for their purpose of winding and binding the great worm; but the mole people were using them now more or less like pikes, guarding the gunwomen behind them.

“They just want to take it down,” Ben said. He climbed out of the drilling machine and approached the melee, but

he had no idea what he could do to help. Zappencackler, the Sphere bearer, and the mole crew followed.

The worm lunged toward the moles, but Violet used careful blasts of the Hand-Held Universal Moisture Remover to stop it. It swayed in place and tried to get at her with its mouth parts. The mole line advanced until it reached the bodies of Fenwick and the fallen mole.

Violet aimed the Hand-Held Universal Moisture Remover at the dead mole person, but then she reconsidered and pointed it at Fenwick, instead. She let loose another conical field of dessication. Fenwick's body dried up in an instant and curled in on itself.

The moles came to a stop. Violet raised the Hand-Held Universal Moisture Remover and aimed it at their front line.

The worm whipped its tail back and forth. Its chiming impacts on the remaining worm tube were the only sounds in the atrium.

The silence held for a long moment until the mole leader called her troops back. They all formed up around the drilling machine for a short conversation of *meeps*, but the upshot was that they all got back inside and – with pointed looks at Violet – they backed the machine up and reversed it down the hole in the atrium floor. Up above, along the galleries, the students raised an enthusiastic cheer.

Ben walked up to the Sphere bearer, who was looking down sadly at Fenwick's mummified corpse. "Sorry about Fenwick," he said gently, reaching out to her.

"He was going to write my Non-Linear Dissolution paper for me," she sniffed.

That reminded Ben where he was. He withdrew his hand.

Up on the worm's neck, Violet was waving the Hand-Held Universal Moisture Remover over her head.

"Can somebody figure out what to do about this worm?"

Ben left Violet at her desk and knocked on the Registrar's door.

"Come in," she called, and so he slipped into her office.

"All done at the Academy," he said.

She was packing a box with keepsakes and whatnot from her desk. "How did it go?"

"About what you'd expect," he told her. "We had a casualty, though."

Registrar Finlay looked up and eyed him. "You don't often have casualties at a lecture," she said at last. "Not at *my* lectures, anyway."

"He bred up some giant venomous worms," Ben said. "One of them got him." This was accurate, if not complete.

"Ah, well. So long as he was the victim of his own experiment. Can you reach those?"

Ben pulled a set of books down off the Registrar's top shelf. "You're... going somewhere?"

"I received an offer from Retropolis Power & Light while I was at the conference today. A very important job. Quite a lot of responsibility, in fact."

She leaned down behind her desk to open a small safe that Ben had never noticed before. From this she pulled out a long, handwritten document. It looked like it had been written by several different people.

"Not to denigrate *this* office, of course," she continued. "Our work here is very important. But when it comes to sheer *scale*, well...."

She settled into her chair and picked up a pen, turning to the latest page in the papers she was holding.

"Shouldn't you get Violet to type that up?" Ben asked.

The Registrar smiled something that wasn't quiet a smile. "No, not this one," she said. "This is just a little guidance the Registrars pass down, from one to the next. We wouldn't want Violet typing *this*."

"Oh, sure, I get it. Privacy."

“Something like that, yes.”

She started to write at the top of a new sheet. Ben was pretty sure he could read Violet’s name, even upside down.

“So,” he tried, “This new job. I guess you got some kind of recommendation?”

“Several of them,” the Registrar replied. She didn’t look up from her writing. “It seems as though all of those speeches and awards and conferences have put me into the... public sphere. I’ve achieved quite a bit of notoriety. Hard to imagine how that may have happened.”

“Hey, that’s great,” Ben said. Then he excused himself and went out to see if Violet’s coffee was ready. It was.

He nodded toward the Registrar’s closed door as he settled into the guest chair. “Looks like we’ll be getting a new Registrar,” he said.

Violet glanced at her row of Employees of the Month. Their faces were still drawn in stark lines of pain.

“How nice,” she said. “It’s always refreshing to have a change.”

“Maybe the new one will promote you.” But Ben was thinking about that long handwritten document, handed down from each Registrar to the next, in which he’d seen Violet’s name.

“I always like to take an optimistic view,” she said. “It’s so much better for one’s state of mind.”

Ben took a long drink of that good coffee. “I couldn’t agree more.”

“Shame about young Fenwick,” he added a moment later.

“That family! Each one brilliant, but they always seem to die so young.”

And that was about all either one of them had to say. So they sat in a friendly silence, with the muffled sounds of the Registrar’s packing coming from behind the door.

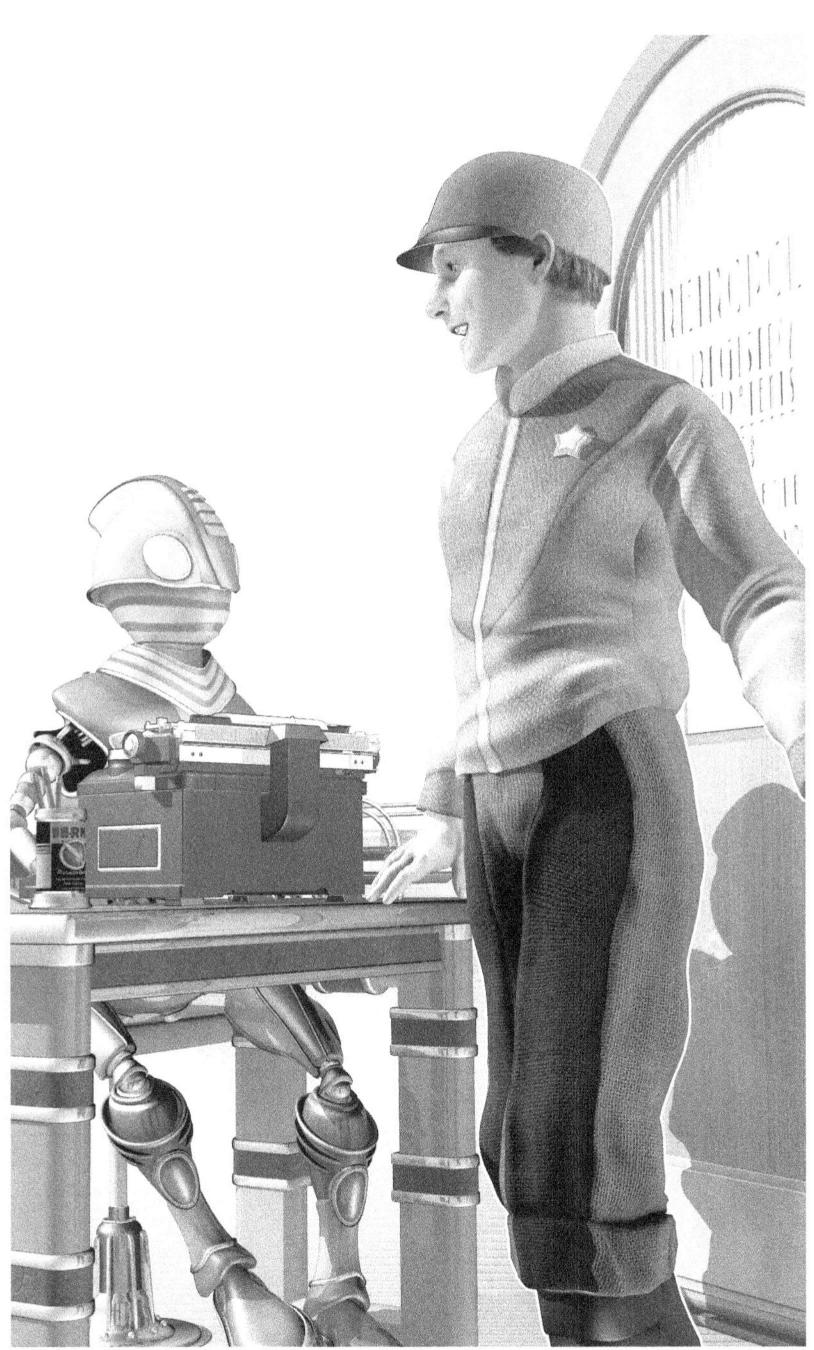

Professor Wilcox and The Floating Laboratory

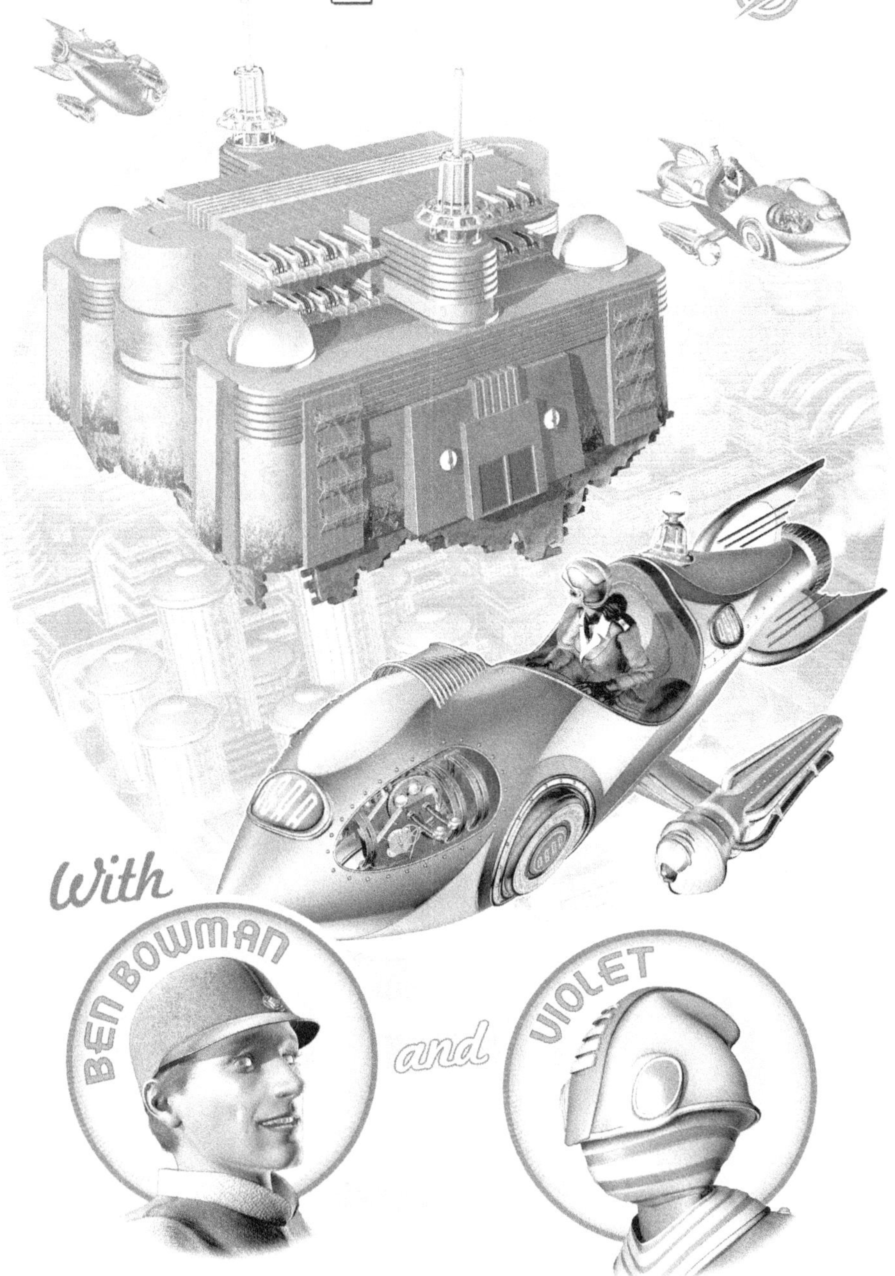

From the files of the Retropolis Registry of Patents

The office of the Retropolis Registry of Patents was nearly always empty when Violet arrived, and she liked it that way. The hallways were silent at that hour, bare tiles empty between the double ranks of the closed, rippled glass office doors. The whisper of her actuators and the quiet clanks of her footsteps were the only sounds in the building. Her glassy eyes glowed softly in the darkness of the empty hall.

At this very early hour it was obvious that the Registry of Patents belonged to Violet. And it was perfectly fine with her that no one else suspected that this was true.

If Violet ruled with an iron hand, that was only to be expected from a robot. But still, one thing had eluded her. One thing – the goal that had motivated her rise to power and her disposal, one by one, of each of the Registrars who arrived with the ridiculous belief that this office was *their* domain – that one thing was still beyond her grasp. Someday she'd be promoted from her post as secretary to the Registrar. Someday she'd become a Patent Investigator. Someday, she was certain, her title would reflect the skills that she'd demonstrated again and again.

Today might be that day.

To understand Violet and her merciless disposition of the Registrars it's important to know how a robot thinks.

A robot's pride and self-image is completely dependent on doing the robot's job. The job must be done; the robot must know that she is in the right place, doing the right thing; and that thing must have been done to perfection. If these things aren't true the robot experiences first discomfort, and then distress, and even actual pain.

It's the worst thing in the world to be a robot that can't do the work that he or she is meant to do.

And why is this? Why do robot brains inflict this kind of punishment on their owners?

The strange truth is that nobody knows. The *even stranger truth* is that nobody knows why robot brains work at all. They *do* work. They're designed; they're built. They work. But the design of robot brains is based on a long process of experimentation. If you assemble the right vacuum tubes, capacitors, and electrical circuits in such-and-such a way you get a robot's brain. Vary those specifications more than a little bit, this way or that, and you get an inert, brain-shaped doorstop.

So you can build a robot that is best suited to be a welder, or a carpenter, or a street cleaner, or an instructor... or a secretary. These problems are pretty well understood. But now and then random chance will step in and a robot will have her own impervious ideas about what she's supposed to do, or who she's supposed to be, and in those cases... look out. You will have a deeply unhappy robot. That is, you will have a deeply unhappy, nearly indestructible, and *unusually powerful* person. You'll be extremely lucky if that person is Violet rather than a giant, heavily armed security robot who would strongly prefer to be a reference librarian.

So it was with a mixture of pride and discomfort that Violet reached her desk, uncovered her typewriter, and poured water, coffee, and something else into the percolator. This was partly traditional – she was still, if reluctantly, a secretary – but the coffee pot was also the magnet that drew Ben Bowman to her desk.

And anyway a new Registrar was expected today, and

some new Registrars drank coffee.

Violet was slipping her private can of motor oil back into a file drawer when the televideo phone rang. This early in the morning, that was likely to be someone calling in sick. So she reached for the schedule before she leaned in to the phone.

Surprisingly, it was Ben Bowman's face that sizzled into view on the screen. He was in uniform, so he probably wasn't going to be using a sick day. Behind him Violet could see traffic flying by overhead: so he wasn't even calling from home.

"Hey, Violet," he said. His voice sounded thin through the videophone speaker. "I beat you in today, just so you know. Wanted to clear my desk before the weekend. You know, that fishing trip next week."

Violet nodded. "Sorry you missed your coffee."

"Yeah, I'll live. Anyway, I'm out by the District already. Going to drop in on Doctor Moore, about that problem with the two preliminaries. Between her and Professor Wilcox. I may be at it all day."

"Well, just be sure you finish by the evening if you want those vacation days, Ben."

She saw his head bob up and down with a lot of vigor. "You bet, wouldn't want to miss it. But there's that other thing."

His face swelled on the phone's screen when he leaned in, one hand cupped over his mouth. Violet did something that another mechanical person would have recognized as a smile. She turned the volume knob down low to help him out.

"It's that new Registrar. He in yet?"

"No, it's just me here," she said.

"Make sure he doesn't open that safe behind his desk," Ben whispered.

She turned the volume back up again. "There's a safe behind the Registrar's desk?"

"Yeah, pretty hush-hush. It's notes the Registrars pass on when you, uh, when they leave."

Violet sank back in her chair. Notes?

"The thing is, Violet, I got a look when Registrar Finlay was getting ready to go. The notes are about *you.*"

I've underestimated them, Violet thought. *Each time I got rid of a Registrar they left... evidence.*

"Did you see how many? Was it all fourteen?"

Ben's face froze. Behind him, a hover sled rose quietly and sped out of the camera's view.

"You've gotten rid of fourteen Registrars? I thought it was... I mean, I only knew about three."

Violet flexed her shoulders in a complicated shrug. "I've been here a long time, Ben."

"Yeah. Uh, okay. Right. Anyway, keep him out of the safe if you want a chance at that promotion."

Violet heard a door open far down the corridor. "That may be him now," she said. "Was there anything else?"

"No, I got to be on my way if I want to go fishing next week. Say... you know, you could come along, if you...."

"I doubt I can get away," she said. "It's nice to be asked, though."

Fish, she thought as she switched off the phone. *What would I do with a fish?* But she was making that secret robot smile again.

She heard a trash can in the hall crash against the tiled floor. "It's so dark in here," someone muttered. "Hello? Is anybody here?"

Violet turned the lights on. "Is that you, Registrar?"

"Yes, I... yes, I suppose that is me," she heard. "Where's my office?"

"You're right in here, sir," she called. "Would you like some coffee? It's fresh."

Registrar Sandrov was enjoying his coffee. He didn't seem to be in any hurry to enter his own office, and they'd been chatting while he relaxed in Violet's guest chair. He seemed pretty interested in her Employee of the Month trophies.

"These are..." He turned the May trophy around. "They seem so...."

"Tormented?"

"Yes, their faces.... And this pattern, running around the feet?"

"Snakes."

Registrar Sandrov set the trophy back down very carefully. "There's something almost...."

"Evil?"

"Well, malicious. It's almost like...."

"Registrar Finlay had a particular sense of humor, sir. She was famous in the office for her practical jokes."

The Registrar looked over at his new office door. Violet slipped a pile of file folders out of her desk drawer. Her moment was coming.

"In fact, sir, I have reason to believe she may have left a... a very energetic practical joke for you. I'd suggest that you never open the safe behind your desk. Not under any circumstances."

"Thank you. I'll, ah, I'll be sure to leave that safe alone."

Registrar Sandrov opened his briefcase and pulled out some papers. "I've been going over the reports. I'm concerned about how few investigators we have just now; we're thirteen short of our average. And the officers, too. We really need to step up our hiring."

Violet pushed her stack of folders a little closer. "That's a real problem," she said. "But they're difficult to train, and if they're not throughly trained they don't do well."

The Registrar shuffled through his papers. "Yes, there was that recent promotion. The fellow from the mail room."

"Officer Binder's retirement seems very peaceful, sir. The home has a large pond. There are a lot of flies in the summertime, but although that would bother most people –"

"Yes. Enough said about that. I hope Officer Binder is enjoying his retirement. Still, that situation makes it clear that officers and investigators must be well trained before we send them out into the field."

While the Registrar stood to pour himself another cup of coffee Violet slid her file folders all the way across her desk. He turned and noticed them.

She pointed helpfully. "On the other hand, we have some experienced help right here in the Registry. I've prepared these files for you, if you have the time."

He smiled. "That's very helpful, Violet. I'm happy to see that you're thinking ahead."

He took the files and started toward the door. "Uh, apart from the safe...?"

"It should be perfectly fine, sir. I tidied up in there yesterday."

He let out a breath and opened the door. "Well, I'll just be making myself at home, then."

Violet watched as the office door swung shut. Then she rose to clean out the coffee pot.

Some would say that the secret to happiness is low expectations. Some of those people would add that it's necessary to lower these expectations on a regular schedule.

None of these people are actually happy. You probably shouldn't listen to them.

Violet, who was also not happy, felt a cautious surge of optimism. She'd deflected the new Registrar from the safe; she'd have to do something about that safe later on, of course, but for the moment its threat had been averted. The files she'd given him were a complete account of all the Registry investigations in which Violet had participated. She was confident that her record would speak for itself. Since the new Registrar seemed like a person she could work with, the future was looking... possible.

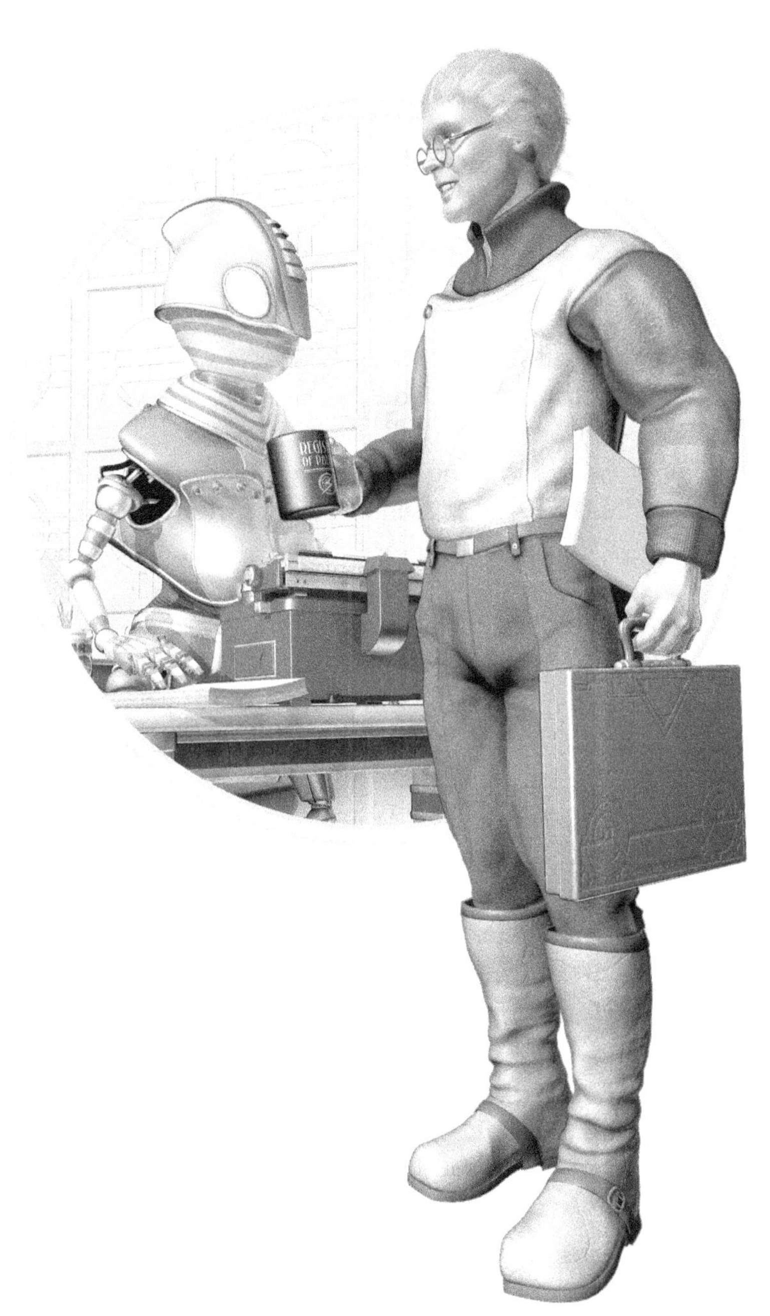

She'd just started a new pot brewing when she heard the televideo ring again.

"Could you pull the files on Professor Wilcox?" Ben's face looked strained. There was a lot of interference in the picture.

"I'll do that right away," she told him. "Is there a problem?"

"Yeah, well, yeah. A problem. Thing is, I was just here for a few minutes when Doctor Moore's laboratory kind of floated away."

Violet reached for Wilcox's file, but that file drawer was just a little too far.

"Floated?" She ducked out of the televideo's view and came back with the Wilcox file.

"There was this big noise, this big *ripping* noise, and everything tilted and shook, and now we're up in the air."

Violet paged through the Wilcox file. "What am I looking for?"

"Something that makes a big ripping noise and sends buildings up into the sky? Maybe?"

"You're sure it's not something Doctor Moore has done?"

"According to her, yeah. I'm, uh, I'm inclined to believe her because she's hiding under a lab table."

Violet scanned Professor Wilcox's patents. "I'm not seeing it here," she said. "I can check his preliminary applications."

"That would be great. Uh, I looked out the window. We're floating over the Switchboard office now."

"You're outside the District?" Violet was shocked. "That's a zoning violation!"

Scientific laboratories in Retropolis are restricted to the Experimental Research District.

"Yeah, well, zoning, you know, not our department," Ben told her. "I'm sure somebody's worried about that. But what we really need here is a way to get down."

Violet thought over the ramifications. "How fast are you moving?"

"What, have I got a speedometer here? I don't know. We're floating. I guess the wind is carrying us along."

Violet checked the weather reports. "Well, you're probably moving at less than ten miles an hour," she decided.

"If you say so. Can you do that check on Wilcox's preliminary patent applications?"

"I'll have to sign off first. They may not be filed yet."

She saw Ben look wildly around Doctor Moore's laboratory. She caught just a glimpse of Doctor Moore herself, under the table.

"I'll call you back when I have anything, Ben. Take care of yourself up there."

She switched off the televideo and thought for a moment. Then she went out into the hall. The officers and investigators had been trickling in.

"I need any recent preliminary applications from Professor Wilcox," she called. "Also, Doctor Moore's laboratory is floating out over the city. It's already outside the District. I'm starting a pool, if anybody wants to bet on where it'll come down."

There was the sound of sudden rustling in offices up and down the hall.

"Where is it now?" somebody yelled. "It looks like the wind is moving at twelve miles per hour."

A head popped out of the office next door. "How much does that lab weigh?"

"Don't forget the preliminaries," she reminded them.

Professor Wilcox hadn't been very active lately, judging by his preliminary applications. Of course there was the one that Ben was investigating, the one that was duplicated in an application by Doctor Moore. Wilcox had filed his *Syncretic Accretion of Non-Flammable Gases in a New Category of Explosion, with Pastry* on the same day as Moore's *Explosive Bimorphism of Inert Gases Within an Edible Shell*, and the two were so similar that an investigation was automatic. In this case, since the two scientists operated next door to one another, the situation was even more suspicious.

But as far as Violet could tell there wasn't any suggestion that *Syncretic Accretion* could be used to lift an entire building into the air except, on a very temporary basis, after an explosion.

Officer Rocklynne brought her two new preliminaries: *Low-Energy Sound Waves Exerting a Remarkable Dissolution Effect* and *Simple Mechanical Implants Which Enhance Leaping Behavior in Squirrels*. No help there, either.

"Three blocks west of the Volto-Vac warehouse on 147th," Rocklynne said.

"What? Oh, yes. The pool."

Violet slid the betting pool out from under Wilcox's preliminaries and added a line at the bottom: *Rocklynne, 3 blks w. Voltoc-Vac on 147th*. She was already on a second sheet, and before long she'd have to add a third.

"Thanks!" said Officer Rocklynne. "Any word on Investigator Bowman?"

"No, he's still trying to figure it out. Bearing up, though. You know Ben."

She slipped the pool sheets back under the preliminaries. "I'm thinking that – if this even *is* Wilcox's work – he must be using something he hasn't registered with us."

"Well, just let us know if there's anything we can do."

She nodded and thanked him. Once Rocklynne had left, she let her eyes wander over the file cabinets. There were just so *many* inventions.

She was still thinking about that when Registrar Sandrov opened his door. "Violet? I was reading those files you gave me...."

She turned to face him. "Yes?"

"Well, I see what you're trying to tell me. If these are accurate – sorry, figure of speech, just procedure, entirely normal – then you're very well qualified to become an officer; probably even an investigator. No question. But I'll need to interview the investigators you've worked with. I think that's mainly Investigator Bowman...? I'd like to talk to him, if he's in the building."

"Investigator Bowman is... not in the office at the moment. I can tell him you'd like to speak to him."

"That would be wonderful, Violet. And I think I can say, procedure notwithstanding, I don't think there'd be any problem. After I talk to Investigator Bowman, I mean."

"Coffee?"

"Oh, yes. Thanks! That's a fresh pot, isn't it?"

"Always, Registrar."

He filled his cup again and went back into his sanctum.

Violet stared at her row of Employee of the Month trophies. After so long, she could hardly believe that this was happening. She just had to get Ben back down out of the air.

Officer Fearn sidled into view, her cap in her hand. "Top of the Constellation Monorail Station," she whispered.

"On top of the station? That's awfully high."

"Yeah, dark horse, I know. But the wind's picked up, and there was a report that the laboratory's gaining altitude."

Violet pulled out the pool and added *Fearn, top of Monorail Stn, Constellation.*

"Thanks!" Officer Fearn disappeared down the hallway.

Violet shook her head. She'd better call Ben. He answered on the second ring.

"Is there any way you can get down, and get back here?" she asked him. "Registrar Sandrov is eager to speak with you."

"We've got six ASAA rockets flying an escort," he said. "But they won't take us off. Some kind of liability thing, with an unmanned building flying over the city."

She had to admit that this was an unusual situation, from an air safety perspective.

"It's really important to me that you speak to the Registrar," she said. "It's about... you know. It's about *that.*"

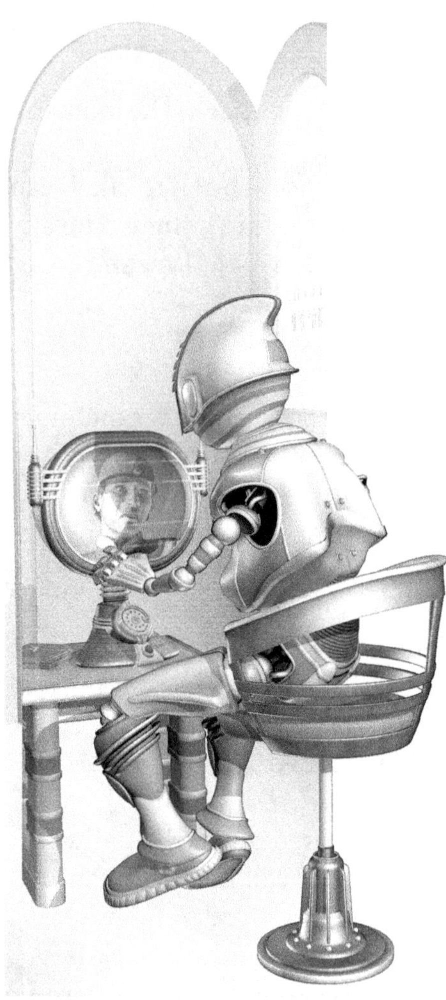

Ben's face, even through the interference on the screen, brightened up into a smile. "Really? Hey, Violet, that's terrific. Just as soon as I get down, I promise. This is... well, it's just swell, Violet. Really happy for you."

He couldn't know that she was smiling back, but she smiled her undetectable smile anyway. "That means a lot, Ben. But we really need to get you out of there."

"No clue in Wilcox's applications, then?"

"I'm about ready to go out there myself. Say... you know, we're running a pool. If you were to start coming down in about forty-five minutes, where do you think you'd land?"

"Let me go check."

Violet watched Doctor Moore's laboratory on the screen while she waited. It was surprisingly quiet, for a flying building.

Ben returned. "In forty-five minutes, we start sinking, I'd say we'd land in the Perisquare. Say... the northwest corner. If we come down slow."

Violet pulled out the betting pool and added *Bowman,*

Perisquare, NW corner.

"There you are," she said. "The pool's up at about a week's pay for you, now."

She saw the laboratory jerk sideways behind him, and Ben tumbled out of view for a moment. "Yeah, well, if you could do something about this, that'd be great. Getting some turbulence up here."

She was just signing off when the Registrar came out of his office again. "I'm really going to miss this coffee of yours," he told her. "Any word from Investigator Bowman?"

"I'm just going out now," she said. "I hope to have him back in about an hour."

"I hope so. I just saw that he's off all of next week, and we'll be seriously short-handed. I'd really like to promote you today."

Violet couldn't speak. She just stared at him.

"So it's important that I talk to him before the end of the day."

She nodded. She still couldn't answer, so she just got up and hurried from the room.

The Registrar grinned, once she was gone. This was his favorite part of any job. Then he glanced down at the papers that were spread across her desk.

She was a good secretary. He really was going to miss her coffee.

No one but Violet seemed to be interested in the empty foundation that Doctor Moore's laboratory had cast off when it reached for the skies. You could see why. On this block alone there was one laboratory that had slumped, recently, into a misshapen pile of stone blocks; there was another former laboratory that had apparently exploded, driving shattered concrete panels into the walls on either side. Laboratories came and went in the Experimental Research District: it's just that normally they went in all directions. Doctor Moore's was the first to decide, for whatever reason, that it ought to go *up*... and stay there.

Someone had capped off the gas main, but the water pipes were shooting a geyser twenty feet in the air and this didn't seem to concern anyone except for some small, orange creatures that were more or less like salamanders. They were swimming and basking in the puddles. Violet took a moment to wonder about the gas and water systems. They were possibly older than the District, since you'd never get a maintenance crew in here to service them. Then she turned to face the laboratory of Professor Wilcox. It was right next door.

Professor Wilcox's lab was built to last, which is typical of the buildings in the District precisely because they never *do* last. Like its neighbors, the building was constructed of huge panels of reinforced concrete that hid its massive slabs of lead shielding. There were some unusual shock absorbers, each about ten feet in diameter, that braced the walls in deep slots that were cut into the laboratory's moat. A narrow walk bridged the moat and met the steps below the blast doors that guarded the entrance. Spidery fire escapes hung optimistically from the roof. On the right side, which faced a new and unscarred lab, Violet saw scorch marks and soot that had penetrated the surface of the concrete and stained it to a darker, smokier grey. On the left, of course, was Doctor Moore's gaping foundation.

Violet made no effort to soften her metallic footsteps on her way up Professor Wilcox's steps. Her feet rang out like trumpets. Her hand, when she pounded on the blast doors, left deep scrapes in their hardened steel. "REGISTRY OF PATENTS," she shouted. "OPEN YOUR DOORS."

After a pause, the blast doors edged slightly open. She could see Professor Wilcox in the shadows within. "You're not in uniform," he said. "How do I know who you are?"

Violet reached straight through the narrow gap and

seized the scientist by the throat. "OPEN YOUR DOORS, YOU FRAGILE HUMAN PERSON."

This was so effective that several other doors opened up along the street. But Violet only cared about the one. As soon as Professor Wilcox had complied, she stepped straight in without releasing his throat.

His feet were trying to get a grip on the floor, but it was hopeless. He ran in place while Violet held him high. She looked at Professor Wilcox's assistant, who was staring at her from the hall. "CAN YOU EXPLAIN WHAT HAS HAPPENED TO DOCTOR MOORE'S LABORATORY?"

The laboratory assistant, who was cowering anyway, shook her head slightly faster than the rest of her body.

"THEN GO."

The assistant went. Violet returned to her examination of the professor.

"Now," she said more quietly, "I'd be grateful if you would explain what you've done to Doctor Moore's laboratory. Then I expect you to reverse the process. One of our investigators is trapped inside. Also, I have personal problems that I want to resolve in a very short amount of time."

The professor denied any involvement with the floating laboratory. "I'd never endanger a Patent Investigator," he insisted. "I depend on my patents... you *know* I do."

"And what about Doctor Moore?"

Professor Wilcox looked down at the floor. "She's... she's not a good neighbor. We've had problems." His eyes came up again and locked on Violet's. "She *stole* my invention!"

"That matter is under investigation," she said reasonably. "We have a system in place. Investigator Bowman was interviewing Doctor Moore when the laboratory... launched."

"Investigator Bowman is in there?" The professor seemed genuinely worried. "I had no idea!"

"WHAT DID YOU DO?"

When she raised him higher and shook him, Violet could see that she had gone too far. He just kept on insisting that he

WILCOX
5943

was innocent of any wrongdoing.

Then the doorbell rang.

At first, Violet was surprised that there *was* a doorbell. But it couldn't be anything else. So she kept Professor Wilcox dangling from one hand and hit the door release with the other. The blast doors swept open to reveal a young woman in Courier Service livery. She had a package, tied with a string, that bobbed lightly overhead. It was about two feet wide and three long, but it was obviously lighter than air – so much lighter that the courier was wearing massive osmium overshoes and belt weights to hold her down.

"Um, delivery for Professor Wilcox?" The courier looked past Violet to see the professor, choking and sputtering, where he hung from the robot's hand. "If I've come at an inconvenient time...."

"You're making an inertrium delivery?" Violet asked.

"Yes, ma'am. Like I was saying, I could always come back later...."

"No, please, don't trouble yourself." Violet looked at the professor. His face was darkening from red to purple. "Would you sign for this package, please?"

Professor Wilcox struggled with the pen and the shipping invoice as Violet continued.

"Have you made a lot of inertrium deliveries to this address?"

"Um, yes ma'am. Every day for, oh, a little over a year now."

The professor handed the receipt to the courier, and she gave him the string. The lighter-than-air metal pulled him upward. Violet heard him gasping for breath now that his weight was relieved. She tossed him down the hall and closed the doors, then made herself useful by carrying the courier's osmium overshoes down the steps. "I'm Violet," she said.

The courier got back on her scooter and unhooked the osmium weights from her belt. There was an inertrium trailer bobbing up behind the scooter, piled with parcels. "Grace Keaton, ma' – Violet. Pleased to meet you."

"I'm with the Registry of Patents. Just a little disagreement."

Grace released her ground straps and the scooter shot upward. She tapped the controls for her upward-facing jets, and the scooter sank back toward the pavement. "I can see how that would happen," she said. "Did you need me for anything?"

"No. Thank you, Miss Keaton." Violet watched as the courier took off *en route* to her next delivery. Then she stepped around Professor Wilcox's laboratory to take a close look at Doctor Moore's foundations.

She found the tunnel without much trouble. It was filled with water from the mains, so she hadn't noticed it before. The tunnel would have opened up into Doctor Moore's basement back when the basement was still there. Violet lowered herself into the water, submerged, and followed the tunnel back to Professor Wilcox's basement. Then she went up the stairs and terrified the professor's laboratory assistant by coming through the basement door. Water poured off her enameled body.

"I need to use your televideo phone," she said. "Sorry about the floor."

"I don't get it." The interference was worse, now, so that Ben's face kept dissolving and reforming on the televideo screen. "He didn't use, I don't know, a graviton dispersal ray? Or a violent reorganization of the atoms under the laboratory?"

Violet looked past the screen so that she could keep Professor Wilcox in view. He was trying to maneuver some kind of cart through the doorway.

"No, he just used a whole lot of inertrium blocks," she told Ben. "Simplest thing in the world. He just added them one by one, each day for more than a year."

Ben's face turned sideways. He seemed to be talking to Doctor Moore. "Could you go look in the basement?" he asked. "There's probably a lot of inertrium down there." He looked back into the screen. "That's kind of disappointing. I mean, it's not what you'd call *inventive*."

Violet kept one eye on Professor Wilcox – because her eyes really could do that – as she answered. "Some say that the simplest solution is the best," she said.

"What? Do they really?"

"Well, the people who say that don't live in the District. But yes, they do. He kept adding the blocks every day until today, when there was finally enough inertrium under Doctor Moore's lab to lift it off the ground. It was just an accident that you happened to be in there at the time."

Professor Wilcox looked up from his efforts with the cart to nod. Then he tried turning the cart to the left. It was pretty well wedged in the doorway.

Doctor Moore's face came into view on the televideo screen. "It's true!" she said. "The basement floor's gone, but the ceiling is packed with inertrium blocks. I showed the ASAA officers."

Ben's eyebrows shot up. "Say, that's great. Are they removing them?"

"Yes. I'm going back down to help." Doctor Moore peered into the camera. "Is Professor Wilcox there? Because I want him to know that I'm going to be *dropping by*."

She headed back to the basement. "I guess I should go down there too," Ben told Violet.

"If you're anywhere near the northwest corner of the Perisquare, Ben, remember that you placed that bet. You could time it just right...."

He grinned. "Yeah, you bet. A week's pay in the pool, right? Then I'll get right back to the office so I can talk you up to the new Registrar."

Violet's invisible smile was back. "Thanks so much, Ben. I'll stay on the line."

She raised a finger at Professor Wilcox. "If you point that thing in my direction I am going to become *extremely annoyed*."

He'd gotten the cart through the door. On one end – the end that he'd been turning toward Violet – there was a peculiar cone, ringed with a spiral glass pipe. The vacuum tubes behind the cone were warming to a golden glow. Green fluid was creeping forward through the pipe.

The professor stopped moving the cart. "You can't just...."

"Oh, I can," said Violet. "You haven't even seen the beginning of what I can do."

It was important that she keep the professor in line, but Violet's temper had cooled once they'd begun the laboratory's descent. She felt that she was nearing the end of a long, painful road: a road that was littered with the scattered careers of former Registrars and paved with the razor-sharp fangs of her own constant distress. By the end of the day she

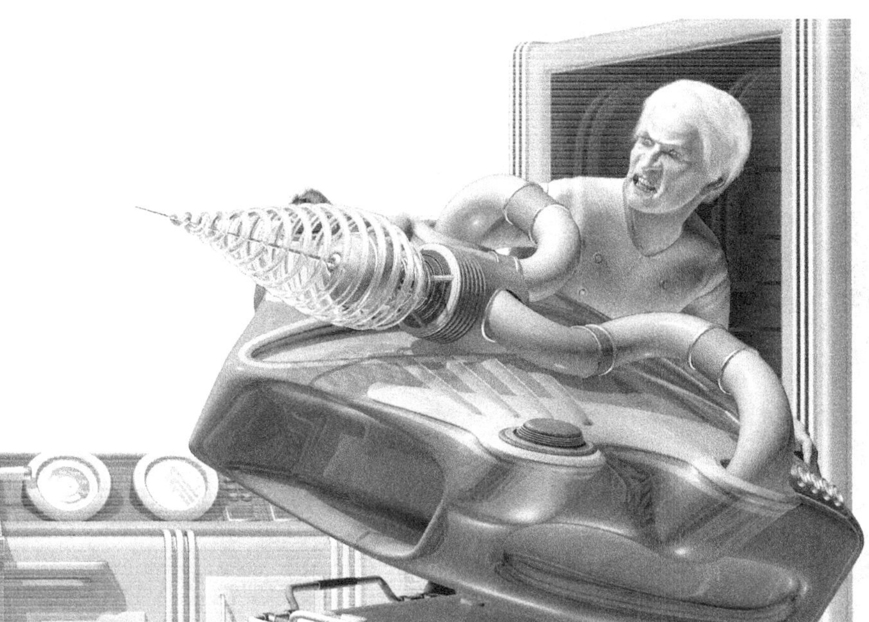

was going to achieve the goal she'd worked so hard to reach. Perhaps she could afford to be generous.

"Just wait a few minutes, Professor, and I"ll be gone. Everything will be back the way it ought to be."

He slammed his palm on the power switch for his device. "Yes, and Doctor Moore will be back next door."

The professor wouldn't enjoy any of the answers to that, so Violet just watched the televideo screen until Ben's face came back into view. "Ha, I think I got it! We were coming down a little too fast, so I stopped shifting those blocks and came back up here to slow things down. I'm pretty sure we'll land right in that northwest corner."

"The ASAA has it in control, then?"

"Yeah, they were kind of upset when I left. But they're doing fine. I mean, if I'd stayed we'd have landed right up by the Trylon. So I think I'm going to win that bet. Smack in the corner."

"It seems like we're both going to have good news today, then."

“Yeah, congratulations. I really mean it. Thing is...” Ben leaned into the camera, running his eyes up and down on his own screen. “...thing is, I don’t think they have a uniform that’ll fit you. Kind of never had to fit a robot before.”

“I’ll just go down to the League of Robotic Persons,” she said. “They have a wonderful body shop there. I’ll get a new coat of paint.”

“Should I be surprised if you’ve thought of everything? Nope.” The laboratory around him shuddered and shook. “I think we just landed,” he said. “Hang on.”

Ben disappeared from view for a moment. She heard him let out a whoop.

She faced Professor Wilcox. “They’ve set down,” she told him. “I don’t know how long it will take to get Doctor Moore’s laboratory back here, but you should probably expect *her* at any time.”

The professor slumped against his cart. “I’m doomed,” he said. “She’s so *good* with toxins.”

Violet told Ben that she’d meet him back at the Registry and switched off. “Professor, get on the line right away and file a complaint with the Zoning Department. If they’re quick they’ll impound Doctor Moore’s laboratory and take her into custody before she can get here. Operating a lab outside the District is a very serious offense.”

His face slowly relaxed into a smile. “Oh. Thank you.”

“If you want to thank the Registry, just keep our investigators and officers out of your neighborhood feuds in the future.”

The professor was happy to agree; Violet was happy to set off for the office and her new investigator’s badge. Everybody was happy, except perhaps for Doctor Moore.

Ben was lingering at the Registry door when Violet came pounding up the steps. “Hey, Violet. Thought I’d wait for you.”

He seemed a little subdued, in the circumstances. They opened up the doors and started down the hall.

"Is everything okay?" she asked. "Did the Zoning Department show up?"

"Oh, yeah. They cordoned off the lab and took Doctor Moore away. Which, you know, it not being her fault, it seemed a little unfair."

There was only so much unfairness that Violet could address in a day. She told him that Doctor Moore would have a chance to defend herself. "But you seem..."

"Yeah, that. It was kind of.... When the ASAA was so hot to keep me down there, bailing out the inertrium. Turns out there was some guy down in the square underneath us. We... we might have missed him, if I'd stayed on the job."

"Oh, that's.... Are you all right?"

"Yeah, it was just sort of a mess. I mean, a whole building. There was only – "

"No, I can't find it either!" said Officer Fearn. She was at the center of a knot of investigators and officers outside the Registrar's office. "I know *I* didn't win, but... Violet! Where were you?"

Everybody turned and glared at Violet and Ben.

Violet peered through the door. The Registrar's inner door was ajar. There wasn't any sign of him inside.

"Where's the Registrar?"

Officer Fearn and her friends wouldn't be distracted. "Where's the pool?"

"It's on my desk, under the Wilcox preliminaries. Hasn't anybody seen Registrar Sandrov?"

"He went out," said Officer Rocklynne. "Said he had to find Investigator Bowman. Found your assignment list with everybody's location."

"My assignment list?" Violet went over to her desk and found the first page of the betting pool on top of the Wilcox files. "I don't have an assignment list. But here's...."

She stood there, perfectly motionless, for a moment. Ben

came over and looked at the pool. Then he pulled a sheet of paper out of his pocket.

"That guy under the laboratory, he was... there was his hand, actually. Not much more. He was holding this."

Ben laid the second sheet of the betting pool on top of the first one. The second sheet was torn and smeared with red.

At the bottom of the page Violet saw her quick notation of Ben's bet. *Bowman, Perisquare, NW corner.*

"Hey!" cried Officer Fearn. "Ben won!"

Officer Rocklynne frowned. "I don't know, with him being on board the thing – is that fair? Couldn't he have –"

The officers and investigators argued about whether Ben's bet had been valid while Ben and Violet stared at the bloodstained sheet.

Very faintly Violet asked, "Registrar Sandrov said he'd found a list of everybody's location?"

Rocklynne broke away from the argument to explain. "Said he was going to talk to Investigator Bowman."

Violet and Ben sank into Violet's chairs. Five minutes later, with the argument over the pool still going, an intern looked in. "Investigator Bowman! There you are. It's five o'clock. Have you filed the complaint report on those preliminary applications from Doctor Moore and Professor Wilcox?"

Ben's face turned toward him, but his eyes didn't focus. "What?"

"Only, it's just you can't take those vacation days next week unless you resolve the complaint. Sorry. You've still got an hour."

Ben shook his head. "Okay."

The intern waited for a moment, but that was all he was going to get. He left.

"So," Ben said to Violet. "It looks like I killed the Registrar."

She nodded. There wasn't much more to say.

"Sorry."

She nodded again. "I know."

RETROPOLIS
REGISTRY
OF PATENTS
OFFICE OF THE
REGISTRAR

The knot of officers and investigators had come to an agreement. “Okay,” Rocklynne said. “So Bowman wins. I still think it’s kind of questionable.”

Violet quietly collected the bets and pushed them, in a ragged pile, toward Ben’s side of her desk. He looked down at his winnings.

“Why don’t you just keep that, Violet?”

“It doesn’t matter, Ben. You take it.”

The others seemed confused that there wasn’t more of a celebration. One by one, though, they dispersed to finish their tasks for the day. That left Ben and Violet, with the pile of money between them, in front of the open door of the Registrar’s office.

They stayed there for a long time.

CLASSIFIED ADVERTISEMENTS

HELP WANTED: Eager, hard working laboratory assistants. No experience required. Meet at the corner of Anisotropic & Incandescence, any morning at eleven o'clock. To preserve trade secrets, tell no one where you're going. See you there!

KITTENS: Five left, beautiful tabbies, calm dispositions. Free to good, non-lunar home. Box 2216

WANTED: STUDENTS FOR ON-SITE SURVEY Just answer twelve simple questions at our offices. Remuneration. Meet at corner of Anisotropic & Incandescence, any morning at eleven o'clock. Research is confidential; don't tell anyone where you're going.

MAKE GREAT MONEY as an Info-Slate switchboard operator. Free instructions: Box 3299

MISSING: 3 engineering graduate students. Last seen at UGRU student union, 10:30 yesterday morning.

CLASSIFIED ADVERTISEMENTS

From the files of the Retropolis Registry of Patents

Ben Bowman came out of the Patent Registrar's office with a can of varnish and a paintbrush. There was a furtive expression on his face. Violet, who was just settling in behind her typewriter, didn't seem surprised.

Not that it's easy to tell – with her being a robot and all – but she hadn't shown any sign of emotion since the day when she and Ben had accidentally killed the old Registrar. It was driving Ben crazy.

"There'll be coffee in a couple of minutes," she told him. He could hear the experimental bubbling of the percolator as it geared up for business.

He sank into Violet's guest chair and watched her sort through the morning mail. The Registrar's In box was taking over her desk since there was still no Registrar to empty it, or to move it into scattered piles inside the office, depending on what kind of new Registrar they were going to get.

Ben waved at the varnish can and the brush. "So, I spent the weekend paneling over the Registrar's safe. Nice work, if I say it myself. I don't think anybody's going to find it again."

Violet just nodded. She didn't look up.

"That means you'll have a clear field, with the new one. None of those old notes, you know, that might set the new boss against you."

The Registrar's safe had contained a fat *dossier* on Violet and her long-running campaign to become a Patent Investigator. If a Registrar didn't want to promote her they always seemed to quit, or lose their position, or get moved to another agency, or (in the case of Registrar Sandrov) die in office. That last one had been a miscalculation: Sandrov had actually *wanted* to make Violet an investigator. It was a real shame, the way he'd died before he could manage it. It was pure bad luck.

Ben wasn't sure that was the way Violet looked at it, though. She hadn't been herself since they dropped that laboratory on top of Registrar Sandrov. It was like she'd... taken it to her electrified robot heart.

He knew that Violet kept a big stack of files that documented all the successful investigations she'd worked. It was already more than some of the investigators had to show for themselves. It *ought* to have been enough to get her that promotion, if it hadn't been for all those notes in the safe.

"You got your files all ready?"

She dropped another letter on top of the Registrar's In pile. "No. I'm not doing that any more."

This was a lot worse than Ben had realized. He started to say something, and stopped, and then he started to say something else, but he stopped that, too. It was going to take some work, turning this around.

The percolator gave a final burp of victory. He went over to the file cabinets to pour himself a cup.

"Anything on the docket for me?"

Violet shuffled through her papers and came up with an assignment. "Officer Rocklynne needs some help down in the Vault."

Ben stared down into his coffee cup. He thought rapidly.

"Maybe Fearn is free...?"

"Officer Fearn is collecting preliminary patent applications all day today," Violet said. "And anyway they always like your input down there. Due to your *unique insight,* according to Officer Rocklynne."

He nodded and drank a third of the coffee in one go. It was excellent, as always. And the insight was hard to argue, since Ben had once studied at the Retropolis Academy for the Unusually Inventive. It wasn't something he liked to mention, but word gets around.

"Uh-huh. Okay, then. Any word on the new Registrar?"

"This ought to be his first day. I'm expecting him... oh, any time now, depending on how long they take over his briefing."

Ben glanced at the clock. He wondered whether he'd rather be here when the new boss arrived, or whether it would be better to head down to the Vault. "The devil you know," he muttered.

"What's that?"

"I said, I guess I should get down to the Vault and see what Rocklynne needs down there."

Violet gave him a look, but then she went back to sorting the Registrar's mail. "There's that new staff down there..." she started.

Ben laughed. "Well, of course there is! Nobody wants to stay down there for long."

"But they're... well, dealing with them requires some care," she said. "Due to their difficult history. As you know, from the –"

He waved her off and rinsed out his coffee cup. "We *all* have a difficult history," he said. "We just have to get up every day and keep going anyhow." He gave her a fierce stare, but this is problematic with a robot. You can never tell what they're thinking behind those still, enameled faces. So he finished with, "If what we want is *worth* wanting, we just have to keep trying," and stalked out of the room.

"Just be careful with them," she said, but he'd left so quickly that he probably didn't hear her. And, anyway, it hadn't been the new Vault staff he was talking about.

She finished sorting the correspondence. There were a dozen inquiries that she could deal with herself, and twenty-two letters that would require the Registrar's personal attention. She rolled a sheet of Registry stationery into her typewriter and looked down at the first letter in her own pile.

She had always been a good secretary: prompt, responsive, motivated, and polite. It's what she'd been built for. And if she had felt that she had a different calling, it had probably been some kind of delusion, or a defect, that she needed to put behind her. Things all made so much more sense this way. She began to answer the inquiry from Doctor Petaja's attorney with swift, crisp punches on the typewriter keys; and if she was aware of her own unhappiness no one could have seen it except, possibly, for Ben Bowman.

She heard footsteps approaching in the hallway, and she stood up behind her typewriter.

"Registrar?"

"Yes, it's me," she heard, and the new Registrar entered the room.

The Vault was known formally as the Patent Registry Models and Samples Repository. But everyone just called it the Vault. It was down below the Registry's offices: very far below. There was a smart way, and a fast way, to get down there. Nobody took the smart way.

So instead of climbing down six flights of stairs, Ben just took the elevator.

There hadn't been a serious incident down here in a couple of years, so the chances that he'd get stuck in the elevator were very small. Once again, the fast way turned out to be the best choice.

Of course once you pass the heavy, shielded doors at the Vault entrance there isn't an elevator any more, and so if you needed to get down to the most recent (and lowest) levels the stairs were your only choice. Ben passed the checkpoints with one finger pointed at his investigator's badge. It was a formality, anyway, but the guards were strict about regulations.

New Patent Officers rotated through Vault duty once a month, but as soon as they got down here they acted the same way that Vault guards had always acted. He'd never figured out how they did that. They seemed perfectly normal once they'd rotated out again.

There were currently twelve Vault levels. The twelfth was still under construction, so Ben knew that he'd find Officer Rocklynne down on Eleven.

What he found first was a crew of child-sized robots who looked like a cartoonist's idea of an ancient Greek warrior. They had heads like stylized helmets. The sweeping, streamlined shapes of their bodies and limbs all looked a little like pieces of armor. Ben had no idea what model of robot they were, but they looked sort of familiar.

The crew was wrestling with a very large apparatus of some kind, spiky with glass tubes and stoppered valves. The robots were making up for their small size through the use of levers and a wheeled platform, but Ben didn't like the way their levers jerked back and forth around the machine's glass tubing.

"Hey!" he said. "We're not playing around here. Be careful!"

The robots froze in place, except for the nearest, who dropped his lever and hid his face. The rest all stared at Ben through their impassive lenses.

He hurried over to pick up the dropped lever. "I'm not kidding!"

The little robots seemed to tense: it was something about the way their shoulders crept inwards while they half-stooped into defensive postures.

Ben handed the lever back to the nearest cowering robot.

"Stowing these inventions is serious business. It's not a *game*."

The robot rushed off toward the stairs while Ben stared after him in disbelief. He turned back to the others, who were still watching him silently.

"Didn't they train you fellas?" he asked. "Didn't they tell you not to horse around down here?"

Another robot broke away and high-tailed it down the corridor.

"Look," he continued, "I'm not trying to scare you. But these things are *dangerous*." He tapped one finger on the machine. "They're not toys."

A third robot dropped his lever and ran, wailing in a soft, melodious voice.

Ben backed away. "Okay, not sure what the problem is here, but just take care with this thing, will you?"

The remaining robots were hunched over, their little eyes blazing with yellow light. They were gripping their levers with a focused intent that Ben was beginning to find unsettling.

"I'll, uh, I'll just go now, then," he said, and that's what he did.

When he saw Officer Rocklynne up ahead, he started to say "What's with the –" but then he saw what Rocklynne was dealing with. "Oh, my."

In most of the area of a Vault level there were rows and columns of shelves, variously sized, and it was on those shelves that the Registry filed the models and samples for every invention that had been patented. The levels were large, and there were a lot of them, but it was the space *between* these working prototypes that was crucial. You didn't want a Transdimensional Magnetic Field Generator anywhere near an Antimagnetic Atomic Repulsor Array, for example; and in fact that *was* the example that was used in the training film that officers and investigators sat through before they were allowed into the Vault. Each prototype was documented and tested before it was assigned a space on the Vault shelves, to prevent the kind of trouble those two devices had caused by their surprising interaction in the Registry's original Vault, which had been located under the Registry's original building.

All this was standard. But there were some devices that just couldn't be classified as safe when they were stored next to *any* other device. These prototypes were stored in sealed, reinforced mini-vaults that were set apart from normal shelving. The mini-vaults had been certified as invulnerable to any existing or any possible contraption. This had always seemed like a tall order to Ben, and Officer Rocklynne was now shoveling sand onto the proof that Ben had been right.

Regulations specified that the free-standing mini-vaults should be built with five feet of clearance between them. It looked like they'd need to amend those specifications sometime soon.

"What are they?" Ben asked.

Rocklynne pointed his shovel at the right-hand mini-vault, whose near wall had crumbled under a thick, oozing layer of blue slime. "Low-Velocity Viscosity Projector," he said. Then he pointed at the mini-vault next door. "And Universal Electron Inverter."

Ben quickly thought through the possibilities if the slime generated by the Low-Velocity Viscosity Projector should ever break down the wall that protected the Universal Electron Inverter.

"That... it might... No. No, I don't know *what* that would do," he said.

"That's why you need to pick up that other shovel," Rocklynne told him. He dumped a shovelful of sand over the slime.

Ben picked up the other shovel and dug into Rocklynne's pile of sand. "Containment Squad coming?"

Rocklynne nodded.

Behind them, Ben noticed that the crew of little robots had caught up to him, shouldering their levers to propel their load. It looked like they were still short-handed.

"You boys doing okay there, now?" he called.

Officer Rocklynne shot him an angry look. "Are you trying to get us killed?"

Registrar Cartier had been very interested in his briefings and he was still paging through the Registrar's manual from time to time while he asked Violet further questions. This was rare, in a Registrar, and it might foretell an enlightened era for the Registry. Violet certainly hoped so.

His only shortcoming was that he preferred tea to coffee. Even the aroma of the coffeepot seemed to trouble him; Violet thoughtfully removed her percolator and left it in Investigator Bowman's office.

The Registrar also wore a rather bold auburn mustache, and Violet saw facial hair so rarely that her instinct was to either trap it or swat it. It didn't look like something that ought to be wandering freely in the Registry offices.

"Very interesting, the Registry," he said as she returned. "Very vital work. Not the simple registration of the patents, I mean, but the oversight over the scientists in the Experimental Research District."

As she slipped into her chair, Violet agreed. "They do take some watching."

"Yes, and dangerous as they are, well! The economic results are so impressive."

She tilted her head. "I'm not sure I…."

"The impact on society! The increased productivity! The innovation, the new industries, the advances!"

Cartier was waving his manual from side to side with every exclamation. Violet nodded, a little unsure where the conversation was going.

"Yes, there *are* benefits. But mostly we try to make sure that they don't send the Earth off into a new orbit, or transform all its water into ammonia. Or something."

The manual waved again.

"And, of course, there are considerable profits to the scientists who make these advances."

"They often don't notice, sir. Increased profits usually go right back into new and better laboratory equipment."

"With immediate benefits to the economy! Their profits

go right back to the manufacturers of that equipment. The whole District is a magnificent money making machine – an engine that drives economic growth."

Violet got up and set a pot of water on to boil. "Well sir, that's a novel way of looking at the Registry's mandate. I have to say, I've seen many Registrars come and go but none of them have taken your particular view of the work."

Registrar Cartier looked thoughtful. "Yes, I noticed that the earlier Registrars all moved on, sometimes rather abruptly. Registrar Finlay..."

"She got a new position with Retropolis Power & Light," Violet said. She returned to her chair and her desk, which stood between her and the new Registrar.

"Yes, and my predecessor..."

Violet's hands flexed over her typewriter keys. "We were all very saddened by the Registrar's death."

"Yes, I imagine. And Registrar Emshwiller..."

Violet's fingers tapped the keys: carefully, because she didn't want to type what she was thinking. Registrar Emshwiller was probably still arranging coconuts into a gigantic 'Help' sign on his tropical beach. "Yes, that was a mysterious disappearance, sir." She *had* sent him a surfboard.

"And then there was Registrar Bergey..."

"Tragic."

"... and, well, you can't forget Registrar Brundage..."

"We try to, sir. Scandal is so very bad for the Registry's image."

He was reciting a list of Violet's forced retirements, extortions, kidnaps, and manipulations: all the acts that had failed, one after another, to bring her the promotion that she'd wanted more than anything. She'd been so desperate to become a Patent Investigator that she'd scattered career after career in a wake of destruction. All of it pointless; all so unnecessary.

She wished he'd just stop.

"It seems as though accepting the post of Registrar sets a ticking clock on one's career, doesn't it?" he said at last.

"I'm sure that's not true, sir. I'm sure you'll do very well in the office."

"Well, I count on you to let me know if any laboratories are about to crash down on me."

There was a quiet moment. "Yes, sir. Let me start your tea steeping."

She rose and moved around him to get at the teapot. It was a little larger than the percolator; she'd have to get used to it sitting there, where the coffeepot had always stood.

Registrar Cartier paged through his manual. "So much to learn, though. So much to learn. For example, what happens when an inventor... well, they don't seem to last very long either, do they? Explosions, sudden liquefactions, unexpected mutations...."

"They've chosen a dangerous line of work, sir. One assumes that they feel a compulsion to do it."

Something like a robot's compulsion to perform what she felt was her vocation.

"Yes, and of course, there are all those benefits, as we've seen. We definitely benefit from their sacrifice. And fortunately the Academy is constantly turning out new scientists to replace the, the..."

"The fallen?"

"Well, yes, that will do. If you like. The fallen."

"But of course our primary role is to make sure their mistakes don't escape the District and cause harm to the rest of the city."

Registrar Cartier poured his tea. "Oh, this smells wonderful, Violet. Very fine." He took a sip, and smiled. "But don't you think our primary role might change? What if we were to, say, encourage certain *types* of research? To keep a closer eye on the more productive inventors, to somehow *guide* them, let's say, toward a more profitable outcome?"

"We've always taken a strictly observational role, Registrar. I think, if you'll forgive me, a thorough reading of Section 128.6(e) might be informative."

The manual snapped shut. "Yes, well, you've been here much longer than I, of course. I'm sure you're right. But coming, as I am, fresh and..."

Uninformed, Violet thought.

"...not burdened by tradition, or by old outmoded ways of thinking, I may have something new to offer the Registry."

"The tea is satisfactory, I hope?"

The Registrar smiled. "Yes, it's very good. Thank you, Violet. I can see that we'll be very happy working together."

"I'm sure you're right, Registrar."

"Oh, and I'm very eager to see this Vault of yours," he said. "Seems fascinating."

"Well, it can be a little... actually, due to the nature our new Vault crew we send everyone to a special training class at the League before they go down there."

She froze. Ben *had* taken the class, hadn't he?

"Oh, a... a class. At the Fraternal League of Robotic Persons? Surely, in the case of the Registrar...."

"It's a very bad idea for anyone to skip the class, Registrar. The Argus crew is quite skillful, but there are certain things one has to be aware of before...."

Ben hadn't taken the class.

"You didn't take the class, did you?"

Officer Rocklynne seemed pretty upset.

"What class?" Ben asked. The little robots were out of earshot, their big load lumbering away toward some distant shelf.

"The Argus class. The one you were supposed to take before you came down here." Rocklynne shoveled another heap of sand onto the blue ooze that was now pouring out of the dissolved wall of the Low-Velocity Viscosity Projector's mini-vault. "They're *Arguses.*"

Ben dumped a shovelful of sand over Rocklynne's. "Right. They're Arguses. Which is, what, a secret society?"

"Don't just shovel that on *my* sand. We need to cover all that slime. No, the Arguses are not a secret society. They're a very old model of robot. There were problems with the Argus line." He distributed some more sand over the outer edges of the mounting ooze. "It was a bad idea to start with. They were built as companions for –" he closed his eyes for a moment, concentrating, and went on: *"human-persons-who-have-not-yet-achieved-their-full-growth."*

"Oh, you mean –"

"Don't say it. Yes, that's what I mean. They were made to be very durable, and they had strict compulsions never to harm

OFFICER

human-persons-who-have-not-yet-achieved-their-full-growth in any way, through action or inaction. Even frustrating a... a person like that... would cause them real pain, the way robots feel when they're not performing their function."

Like Violet, Ben thought. He shoveled some more sand over the other edge of the ooze. "Sure, okay. Not to harm or even frustrate –" Rocklynne held up a finger. "– a person of that description. A *shorter than usual* person?"

"Specifically, *human-persons-who-have-not-yet-achieved-their-full-growth.* Other people are short too, you see."

Ben nodded. He picked up some more sand, but they were starting to run low; the blue ooze, on the other hand, looked to be picking up steam. "Hope that Containment Squad gets here soon. So, okay, it makes sense: they're meant to pl–"

"*Don't say it.*"

"That is, they're meant to, uh, interact in a lighthearted way with *persons of that description.* So the builders made sure they couldn't ever harm those persons. What's the problem?"

Rocklynne wiped his forehead. He was also looking at their dwindling pile of sand. "Well, I guess the designers of the Argus line had never seen an actual *person of that description.* When the robots went out to, uh, do what they were meant to do, they ended up in all these scenarios like fiery rescues, underwater captures, chemical experiments, full-on war... simulations, battles to the death...."

Ben thought back on the kind of games he'd played with his own toys. "Oh. Yeah. I think I see the problem."

"And the Arguses could only feel satisfied by doing their job, right? Which was basically to be tortured all day, every day. And they couldn't fight back, or even raise an objection."

"Yeah," Ben said. "You take your cat, like. You play rough with it, it's got those claws and teeth. You figure it out." He picked up another shovelful of sand.

"Exactly. So there were... there were these incidents. Only about twelve per cent of the time, but still...."

Ben stood up straight. "No! They didn't hurt the –"

"*Don't say it.* No. But the designers didn't put in those kind of constraints when it came to adult human persons. Right? And you set up that kind of situation, something's going to give. Something's going to crack."

Ben looked up and down the corridor. He though he could hear those little metallic feet on their way back. "Yeah, I get it."

"So the whole line was recalled, except for a few that... went rogue. Disappeared. And over time the League was able to make some slight changes to the Arguses', you know, psychology or something, so that they could feel useful by doing other forms of work. But they can't ever come into contact with *human-persons-who-have-not-yet-achieved-their-full-growth*, and you have to exercise a lot of discretion when you talk to them. Some words, you know, they just bring back all those horrible experiences, and there's always a chance – it's a small chance – that one of them will crack because of the memories. But they're really good workers. They really want to do their jobs. You know, especially Bonkadoo and Wapfangle, they're–"

Ben was really trying not to crack up, but there are limits.

Rocklynne glared at him. "They're just names, all right? Get over it. Anyway, a couple of them are showing real potential as leaders. The work program's been a big success. And this is a great place for them, because *persons of that description* never come down here, and so few of us are authorized to come to the Vault that it's easy to make sure we all get the training."

"Yeah. I think maybe Violet kind of made a mistake, there," Ben said. "That's not like her, but she's been, you know...."

Rocklynne nodded. "Yeah. We all know. Anyway, most of the training is about the words you can never say."

He looked toward the distant sound of Argus footsteps. Then he leaned in and whispered: "Words like *boy* or *girl, child, kid,* or *children, game* or *toy* or *play*. Like...." He was looking into Ben's face, which had suddenly gone blank. "No. Tell me you didn't."

"I guess I... yeah, most of those, I think. Also 'horsing around'."

Rocklynne shook his head. "You probably shouldn't talk to them *at all.* And 'horsing around'? I mean, I've never even understood what that *means.*"

"It means –"

"*Don't say it.*"

Ben dragged his shovel through the last of the sand pile. "It's strange. I've never even heard about these fellas before."

"It was a long time ago," Rocklynne told him. "It's taken decades to get them over the worst of it, so they could come back into the world. Even a little bit."

Ben pointed at the broken wall of the Low-Velocity Viscosity Projector's mini-vault. "That stuff is really pouring out now," he said. "Have we got any more sand?"

"A couple of buckets, three rows down," said Rocklynne. "I don't know what's keeping that Containment Squad."

"There were some delays in the monorail system this morning," Ben remembered. "Maybe they got stuck somewhere on their way to work."

It wasn't a bad explanation. It was just completely wrong.

Officer Bok rushed to Violet's desk with bad news. "Something's gone wrong down on Vault Eleven," she said. "Rocklynne called for the Containment Squad. But they can't get through because there's some kind of obstruction at the end of the stairwell."

At moments like these the only sound in Violet's reception area had once been the gentle bubbling of her percolator. But the percolator was gone now.

There wasn't any sound at all while Violet took in the news and tried to imagine the scope of the disaster.

"Did Officer Rocklynne say why he needed the Containment Squad?"

Officer Bok shook her head.

"Get an Info-Slate from the supply room and get down there, would you? I'll check out another one so we can keep in touch. And... don't worry, Hannah. Ben's down there too. It will probably be fine."

But Ben may have *been* the problem. As Bok hurried out, Violet looked down at the class roster. There wasn't any question: she'd sent Ben down there with nothing but a vague warning. And although the Argus work program had been successful, nowhere in their assignments around the city had the reconditioned robots been exposed to human persons who weren't trained to deal with them.

She had to inform the Registrar.

At first she knocked as softly as she could on the door frame (an acquired skill, for a person whose fingers were made of metal), and then she rapped a little louder, and a then bit louder again, before she heard the Registrar's "Yes?" and opened the office door.

"There's a bit of trouble down in the Vault," she explained. "It probably won't be serious, but there's a chance we'll need to evacuate the building."

Registrar Cartier blinked.

"I'll let you know if things get dangerous down there."

"Yes... yes, thank you."

He had been working his way through a stack of patent registrations. Violet saw that his In box was still overflowing with mail. "Anything I can do to help?"

"Well, when you get a chance... I'm still curious about those inventors who've died. Could you...?"

"I'll get you the last, say, six months' worth of deceased scientists?"

"Yes, that would be perfect, Violet. Thank you."

"May I say, sir, that you show admirable restraint for a Registrar whose building may be on the brink of destruction?"

"Oh, is that unusual? I assumed this sort of thing was normal around here."

"I'll get you those files. But have you noticed the letters from the Fourth Circuit Court? They seemed to be quite impatient for a reply."

"Oh, well." Registrar Cartier waved one hand. "I won't keep them waiting long."

"I'll type the letter whenever you're ready, sir."

Dismissed, she closed the door gently and set off for the supply room to pick up an Info-Slate. With that in hand she

worked through the file cabinets, gathered together the files for the most recently deceased District scientists, and handed most of them to Irving, a nervous Beetlebot who needed something to do. Then she thumbed on the Info-Slate.

Info-Slates were common in the higher profile city departments, like the Air Safety and Astronautics Association or the Retropolis Department of Power and Light. At the Registry of Patents, though, there were only a few of them.

Violet looked over the several panes of information on the device's face. She thumbed a dial, and selected something by accident: somewhere across the city she knew that an operator was noting her selection and swapping cables to connect Violet's Info-Slate to what turned out to be a list of properties from the Zoning Registry. Violet winced and made a silent apology. What she really wanted was in a larger pane near the top of the device.

Officer Bok's Info-Slate appeared there in a list of connected devices, so she thumbed her way to that entry and pressed a button.

"Gaaaaahhh!" said Hannah Bok's voice. Officer Bok was even less experienced with the Info-Slates than Violet.

"Officer, it's Violet. Have you reached the Containment Squad?"

All Violet could see in the televideo panel was Officer Bok's hip.

"Could you look into the camera, Officer?"

"Where's the camera?" asked Officer Bok's hip.

Once she'd worked out where the camera was, things went a bit more smoothly.

By peering at the Info-Slate's televideo screen, Violet could see the Containment Squad shuffling, sitting and fidgeting at the entrance to Vault Eleven, where they'd been stopped by a wall of piled-up machinery that blocked the door. Faint sounds of activity seemed to come from the far side of the barricade.

"There's no way to push through it?" Violet asked.

"No, and the fact is, none of us wants to even touch that stuff. Can't you see? It's wall of prototypes. They're all just wedged on top of each other, maybe six feet deep. If we should turn any one of them on by accident...."

Even powered down, those machines shouldn't have been anywhere near each other. "Yes, I see."

Officer Bok's face wavered back into view on the screen. "No word from Rocklynne or Bowman. We just don't know what's going on in there, Violet."

"Does the Containment Squad know why Officer Rocklynne called them?"

Officer Bok's face vanished, and the squad leader appeared. "He reported a breach in one of the mini-vaults.

Some spillover, not sure what it is. Seemed to be threatening the next vault over."

Violet's finger tapped the side of the Info-Slate. This was bad.

"And there's been no more contact with him?"

The squad leader jerked his thumb toward the stairwell's wall, where Violet could see a televideo set. "That's the only videophone on the level. You know the regulations."

He was right. There were stringent limits on what kinds of devices could be taken into a Vault level. Mostly, the list said "none".

So with no way to get in, no way to contact anybody inside, and no way to know how bad the situation was, there wasn't any doubt what would happen next.

"I'll start the evacuation," Violet said.

Ben and Officer Rocklynne looked down at the three remaining buckets of sand. "Well, that's not going to go too far," Rocklynne decided.

They were off in the shelves, several rows away from the fractured mini-vault. There were sand buckets spread throughout the level, but they'd just about exhausted the whole supply. Meanwhile the Low-Velocity Viscosity Projector continued to seep its slimy blue ooze at an increasing rate.

"Okay," Ben said. "What if we forget about the sand and just open up one of the mini-vaults and move a prototype way the heck out of there?"

"Not the Low-Velocity Viscosity Projector."

"No, we don't want any of that blue goop to get on us, either. We move the Universal Electron Inverter."

Rocklynne kicked one of the sand buckets. "Any idea how big it is?"

"I know how to find out."

So they left the sand buckets where they were and headed

back to the mini-vaults. Just as they neared them, the crew of Arguses reappeared. They'd deposited their load on some faraway shelf and now they trudged back toward the stairs with their levers over their shoulders.

"Say, fellas," Ben called. He ignored Officer Rocklynne's glare. "We're going to have to move that Universal Electron Inverter down the way. Want to give us a hand?"

The little robots stopped. They didn't say anything; they just stared at Ben.

"Then, maybe, after, well, I see you've got like a whole baseball team there. We've got a pretty good team of our own, upstairs. Maybe we can get together for a g– "

Rocklynne's elbow smacked into his ribs. The robots hunched over into their defensive postures again. Most of them dropped their levers, and then they rushed away down the row toward the level's entrance.

"You are just about the stupidest smart person I've ever met," Rocklynne told him.

"It was just baseball," Ben complained. "Everybody loves baseball."

"And anyway, what was that about having enough for a team? You only need nine for a team."

"Well, there's nine of 'em."

They arrived at the Universal Electron Inverter's mini-vault. Officer Rocklynne paused. "Then what happened to the other three?"

Ben entered his code on the mini-vault's keypad and laid his hand on the hatch. "I, uh, I think three of them may have run off earlier," he said.

"You know it's going to take them a week to get over this, right? My advice, you don't say another word till you get out of the Vault."

"You bet," said Ben. Then: "Oh, well, here's a problem." He was looking into the mini-vault. "So that's what a Universal Electron Inverter looks like."

A Universal Electron Inverter looks like something that's

very heavy without surrendering anything in the way of breakability. This one was a curious combination of squat legs, fragile glass jars, a generous and most likely essential complement of lead shielding, and one dimly glowing sphere suspended in the middle, apparently held immobile by magnetic fields. It must have had some kind of battery power because there was a quiet, self-satisfied hum coming from the central sphere. A spigot jutted out from the juncture of six hoses.

"Well... we've got those levers, I guess. And there might be a pallet around here someplace."

Ben shook his head slowly. "Yeah, could be." He looked up and down the row of shelves. "Could be."

There was a sudden *blurp* from the mini-vault next door, the one that was no longer containing the Low-Velocity Viscosity Projector. About three gallons of glowing slime oozed out over their pile of sand and slowly flowed toward the Universal Electron Inverter.

"See if you can get behind it in there," Ben said. "I'll go look for a pallet."

Incredibly, there was a pallet. There were even some spare blocks of inertrium floating on lines tethered to a nearby shelf. So however heavy the Universal Electron Inverter was, they'd probably be able to move it if they could just shift it onto the pallet first. Things really seemed be be looking up until Ben brought the pallet back to the mini-vault.

Officer Rocklynne hadn't worked his way in behind the Universal Electron Inverter because there just wasn't enough room to get around it. So they went back to get the extra inertrium blocks, one by one because they didn't want to float up to the ceiling, and they started to tie them to the legs on the Universal Electron Inverter's near side.

The legs began to lift. It was a slow job.

Blurp. Rocklynne went back to get another block of inertrium. The Universal Electron Inverter's legs were about halfway high enough to slip the pallet under them

Blurp.

Blue slime was edging toward the Universal Electron Inverter's vault. It was just inches away.

"What you said back there, about Violet?" Ben said. "You said *we all know.*"

"Everybody knows she wants to be an investigator. It's just a shame, how all these Registrars come and go, and none of them staying long enough to get to know her."

"Well, Finlay lasted a few months."

"Yeah. Well, she needs some time with the *right* Registrar, I guess."

"And that's what you meant, then? About *we all know*?"

"Yeah, what else?"

Ben was relieved that *we all know* didn't cover the fates of the Registrars who hadn't promoted Violet. "Okay," he said. "That's done. Let's get a couple more blocks."

Blurp. This time, they ran.

As they tied the new blocks to the Universal Electron Inverter's legs, Officer Rocklynne added: "You know we'd all help her, there was anything we could do. It's swell, the way you've been with her."

Ben shrugged. "Hey, Violet's my pal."

"Yeah. I guess that's it. Here, let's see if we can get it onto the pallet now."

They heaved on the Universal Electron Inverter's frame and got its near legs just onto the edge of the pallet. *Blurp.* Each of them grabbed a leg and they pulled together. The big, heavy machine moved about a quarter of an inch. They took deep breaths and tried again. It shifted again, but not quite so far.

The blue slime was beginning to pool at the mini-vault's base. It was making a hissing noise.

"If I could just get in behind it and push," Rocklynne panted.

"You know what we need?" Ben said. "It's those little Argus guys."

Rocklynne let go of the Universal Electron Inverter's leg. "Yeah," he agreed. "I wonder where they are?"

Registrar Cartier wasn't very cooperative, as evacuees go. First he insisted on getting a cart for his files. Then he ran back for the Registrar's stamp, a big embosser on a heavy, arched stand. After that he wanted to save some of the other files, and through it all he never even remembered his unanswered correspondence. Violet slipped the In box into his cart while he wasn't looking.

But finally she managed to get him out of his office, down the hall, and onto the front steps of the Registry building. "Honestly, Registrar, this isn't far enough. We should get you at least as far as the street."

Registrar Cartier looked at his cart, and then at the building, and then at the cart again. "I... suppose so. But I don't feel right about abandoning the Registry." He reached down and touched the Registrar's stamp. "On my first day, especially. There's so much *potential.*"

"Some of our best people are down in the Vault," she reminded him. "And there's nothing you can do from here."

"I'll just stay here a little longer," he said, and there wasn't much more she could do. So she reconnected with Officer Bok on the Info-Slate.

It looked as though the Containment Squad was working on disassembling the wall of prototypes. This was made more difficult – and, probably, more dangerous – by the fact that they didn't know what any of the prototypes were. This was an area where Violet, with her capacious memory, was able to assist.

"Can you hold the Info-Slate a little higher? Yes, that's it. That device on top is Doctor Pohl's Constantly Emanating Emulsifier. It's perfectly safe to handle, so... yes. Then right below it is something that looks like Professor Fenwick (III)'s

Excitingly Silent Neural Nebulizer. It's off, right? *Don't turn it on.*"

"Professor Fenwick (III)?" said Registrar Cartier. "I think I have that one here." He paged through the files he'd brought down in his cart. "Yes, I thought I remembered the name."

"You'll have a lot of Fenwicks in the deceased files," Violet told him. "It's a large family, and they never seem to... Officer Bok? Tell them not to touch that one. We'll want to look it up." She tapped on the controls for her Info-Slate's lower pane. There was a brief delay while the faraway operator switched the cables, and then a list of Patent registrations appeared. Registrar Cartier leaned over her shoulder.

"That's a remarkable device," he said. "I don't suppose that I have one?"

"We have just four," she replied. "Officer Bok? Tell them *not* to touch that one, not under any circumstances. In fact you shouldn't get any exposed skin within... oh. Oh, I see. You should take that to the medics in about an hour. You'll be fine till then, and anyway it'll grow back."

There was a unidentifiable noise coming from her Info-Slate. "No, really, it's not that serious. Tell the Containment Squad to leave that column alone. But if they start at the top, over to the left...."

"I've heard good things about these Info-Slates." The Registrar's face was hanging over Violet's shoulder, and he was standing very, very close to her. That would have been odd even without the presence of his mustache, which was quivering silently on his upper lip. Her eyes fixed on the mustache. She couldn't look away.

"Yes, Registrar. As I said, we just have a few of them." She forced herself to look away from the mustache, and turned back to the Info-Slate. "Yes, that one's safe. I remember that one." She could imagine the mustache nodding slightly in agreement, right behind her.

"So you can sort all the registered patents, I take it, according to different criteria?"

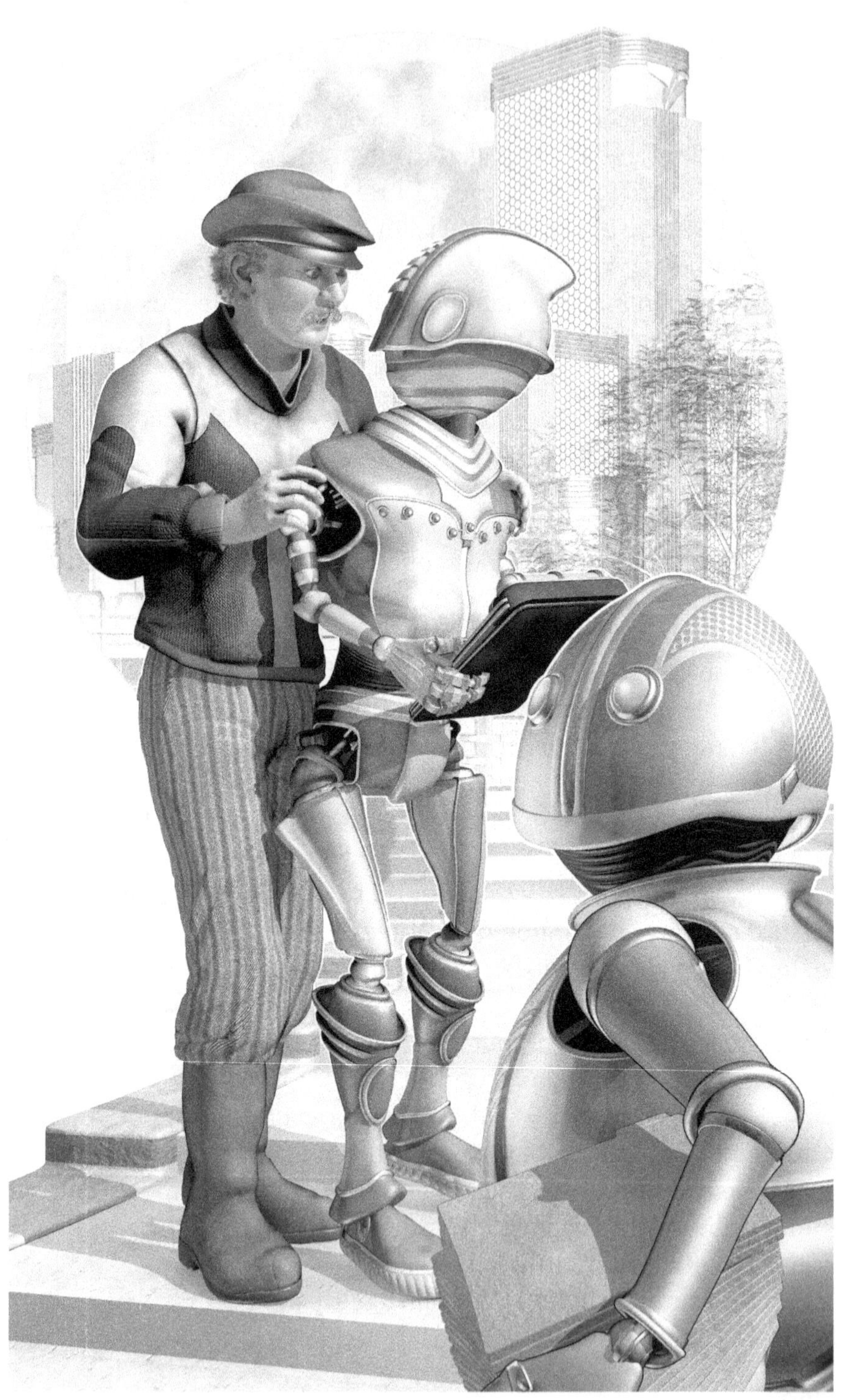

She nodded.

"So if I wanted a display of patents registered to inventors who are now deceased...?"

Violet glanced at his cart full of the files for deceased scientists. "Yes, that would be simple, Registrar. But at the moment we're..."

"...quite busy. Yes, I see. Please don't mind me."

She did her best not to mind him while she identified one device after another for the Containment Squad, who lifted the machines cautiously from the heap and laid them on the stairs.

"Hang on," said Officer Bok through the Info-Slate. "Look at that first column!"

A new device had appeared in the gap they'd been carving in the wall of prototypes. Then, just above that one, a new and frighteningly dangerous machine slid into position. The wall was sealed up again.

"Stop!" she said. On the Info-Slate screen she watched as the Containment Squad backed away from the wall.

Whoever had built the wall of prototypes was closing it back up, just as quickly as the Squad was taking it down. "There's no telling what they'll shove in there next," Violet explained. "We're only making things worse."

"May I?" asked the Registrar, and she handed him the Info-Slate. He started to experiment with the list of registrations. "Yes, a wonderful device," he said. "We should get more of these."

"Well, it's the expense, Registrar. We could only get a few of them."

"Oh, a new day may be dawning, Violet. I intend to make the Registry a profitable enterprise."

This stopped Violet short in spite of the dangerous situation down below their feet. "The Registry making a profit, sir? I'm not sure that's possible. And, anyway, our mandate is to record and –" she looked around; only Registry personnel were within earshot. "– to, well, monitor the activities of the

Experimental Research District. Our budget...."

Registrar Cartier laughed. "Oh, of course. Our mandate. Don't worry about it, Violet. My management style isn't like what you've seen before. That's all. Just sit back and let your manager manage."

"It's just that... the ordinances, sir, that established the Registry. We're a fully funded branch of City Government. There's simply no provision for revenue."

"Yes. The ordinances. Well, let's say I have some philosophical differences with *fully funded* civic organizations. Every branch of City Government should support itself, and in fact should generate income. In a sane society, that would always have been the case."

Under different circumstances Violet might have brought up firefighting, sewage management, streetlights, medical care, education, and a couple of dozen other functions of City Government that, in a sane society, could *never* generate revenue. But she had other problems to deal with, so she just asked him for the Info-Slate. Through its televideo display she could see the despondent Containment Squad scattered around the stairwell. Officer Bok had set her own Info-Slate down on the steps.

They weren't going to get through from the stairwell side; that much was clear. What hopes they had must rest on Ben and Officer Rocklynne. Violet wished she had some idea of what was going on down there.

"What do you think they're doing?" asked Ben.

He and Officer Rocklynne had reached the end of Level Eleven's rows of shelves and mini-vaults. Where the door to the stairwell should have been they saw a large rectangular enclosure built from piles of the devices and demonstration models that used to be shelved carefully to either side of Rocklynne and Ben, but were now heaped up into walls that had terrifying possibilities.

Rocklynne was staring at the wall. "I think they built themselves a fort."

Down at the fort's base, a rectangular device slid out of sight. This allowed one of the Argus robots to shove a new prototype inside. Once he'd followed it inside the fort, the rectangular object slid back into place.

"Maybe we should have given them a couch," Ben mused. Rocklynne's eyebrows performed a complex maneuver. "You know, they make great forts. When I was a –"

"*Don't say it.*"

"Yeah, right. Anyway, your couch, it's terrific fort material. Much better than...." Ben waved at the precarious walls.

"Well, this could be worse," said Rocklynne.

Ben wasn't sure how. Behind them, the Low-Velocity Viscosity Projector was slowly seeping into the walls of the Universal Electron Inverter's mini-vault; ahead of them, the Arguses had piled several thousand pounds of dangerous devices on top of each other without any regard for the ways they might interact. It was hard to guess which situation would be the first to kill them all.

"I mean, what they're doing, it's *defensive*. They're trying to protect themselves from you. Whereas, you know, they might have gotten more *aggressive*, and if they'd done that then you'd be dead now. Me too, maybe."

Ben nodded, glum.

Rocklynne ignored him. "'Course it's all moot, really. We've got a time bomb behind us, and that fort... well, I've got no idea what's going to happen there. You see that Anamorphic Matter Reformulator? I'm pretty sure it's not supposed to be glowing like that. And that, just beside it? I'm thinking that's a Hydrophilic Isolation Tank. Which, depending on what's inside it...."

"Yeah, it looks like they switched it off. So we'll probably find out soon."

The two of them thought about their situation.

"You ever designate a beneficiary for your insurance?" Ben asked.

"Yeah. You?"

"I was going to."

They thought some more.

"Thing is," Ben said at last, "we don't really need the little guys right now, like we thought we did. I mean, I bet the Containment Squad's on the other side of that wall. Explains why they never got here. And those are the guys we really need. With all their fancy equipment."

"Your point?"

"Well, it's just not the problem we thought it was, right? We don't need those Argus fellas to *help* us. We just need to get them out of the way."

"You're talking about a dozen mentally unstable robots who are surrounded by piles of machines that might start exploding, any minute now," Rocklynne reminded him. "So you want to, what, push them out of the way?"

Ben was frowning. His face was pointed toward the Argus robots, but his eyes weren't focused. "What was that thing you called me?" he asked.

"At this point I am not sure how many things I've called you, or what they were. And that's just the things I said out loud."

"You said I was the stupidest smart person you've ever met."

"That's the least of it. And what I actually meant to say was –"

Ben waved his hand. "Not important."

"– that you were grossly insensitive about these little robots and what they've been through. That you're a big –"

"No, the first one was the good one. Though *grossly insensitive*? That's not bad. I'm thinking that's exactly what we need. And the other one... the thing about the Arguses and *human-persons-who-have-not-yet-achieved-their-full-size*. That's the other thing."

"I have no idea what you're talking about," Rocklynne told him.

"That's okay. I'm going to do something really stupid now."

He stepped forward almost quickly enough to miss Rocklynne's "Yes, of course you are." But Ben's mind was still on what he needed to say. It had to be just right.

No. It had to be just wrong, in just the right way.

High above, Violet was trying to decide whether there was any point to keeping the Containment Squad in the stairwell. There was no need for them to die down there. It didn't seem like there was any chance that they could fix whatever was going on down on Eleven. But she figured that this was a question for the Registrar.

He had the Info-Slate in his hand. He seemed to be fascinated by the thing, with its easily sorted lists of just about everything. It wasn't easy to get his attention; but, as it happened, Officer Bok managed it with an insistent *beep* that came from the Info-Slate itself.

"Something's happening," she said through the Info-Slate speaker. "I think somebody's in there. *Talking.*"

"Who do we have in there?" the Registrar asked.

"It's Investigator Bowman and Officer Rocklynne," Violet said. "They're, uh, they're very fine people."

And half of them have taken a class in how to deal with Argus robots, she added to herself. But she had a feeling that it was the other half who was doing the talking.

"Hey, little guys," Ben started. "Um, that's a great fort you've got there. But, you know how this level is full of machines that shouldn't be stored anywhere near each other? Well. Those are the machines you just stacked up all around you. The ones that shouldn't get close to each other."

He could see the Arguses' yellow eyes gleaming in the gaps between the prototypes.

"Which is what you would call an extremely dangerous situation, is what I'm saying. And I do not want to alarm you in any way, but, like I said, extremely dangerous."

He stepped up and stopped about eight feet from the fort's near wall.

"So the smart thing would be to very carefully take these walls apart and move all the prototypes away from each other. That would be the smart thing, here. Because any one of them, for example that Triphasic Gaseous Recombinator, might go unstable and set off a chain reaction that would probably destroy this building which we are in. Which, I mean, we are underneath. And everybody who's upstairs? They're goners, too."

There was a quiet, rustling sound inside the fort. The little yellow eyes didn't blink; but, then, they didn't blink anyway. So Ben wasn't sure if he was getting through.

"So that's our first problem. The incredibly unstable wall of things that should never be put next to each other. That one's pretty bad. But hang on: there's more. 'Way back behind us there's this Low-Velocity Viscosity Projector, which has eaten through its mini-vault. It's seeping corrosive slime that is just about ready to eat through the mini-vault next door, which contains the Universal Electron Inverter. And, you know what? I have no idea what's going to happen when the one comes into contact with the other. All I know is that each one of those devices is so dangerous that we decided to put them into these impervious vaults which are, ha ha, not quite as impervious as we thought they were. So, best guess, when the ooze from the Low-Velocity Viscosity Projector hits the Universal Electron Inverter, everything on Level Eleven goes bang. Which includes all of us, right?

"But more to the point, when Level Eleven disappears then all the levels overhead come down on top of it, which is also likely to be a disaster, and which will certainly kill everybody in the building on top. *Everybody*. Okay?"

More pairs of eyes were peering through the wall. Ben had an urge to wave at them, but he resisted. The situation called for dignity.

"And all of that is pretty bad. I mean, your fort here, it's likely to kill everybody upstairs when it blows, and then the Low-Velocity Viscosity Projector and the Universal Electron Inverter will kill us all. I mean, they'll kill us all over again. And everybody in the Registry building above us? They're all dead, too. Twice over."

He paused, purely for effect, because what was coming up was either the smartest or the stupidest thing he had ever said.

"And that's a real shame, you see, because today is the day that four whole classes of *boys* and *girls* are getting a guided tour of the Registry."

Something dropped inside the fort. It rolled a long way in the silence before it bounced off a wall and came to rest.

"That's, I figure, one hundred and twenty *children* who are about to die, and I mean, really horribly, and all because you built this fort down here on Level Eleven. Yep, those poor *kids* just came to learn about the Registry, thinking it was, like, educational. All those *boys* and *girls* would rather be out in the park. But all *one hundred and twenty children* are about to die unless you take your fort apart and let the Containment Squad through."

He waited. "The thing I'm saying is, because of what you've done dozens of *kids* are about to die. And they're, uh, *children*. Just *children*."

That was all he had. Ben stepped back to join Officer Rocklynne.

"Even if this works," Rocklynne hissed, "I'm not sure there's any excuse for it."

"We might all live," Ben offered. "And like you said, they can't do anything that will hurt children. I just encouraged them, you know, to act according to their nature."

"You hear anything about this new president over at the Fraternal League of Robotic Persons?"

Ben hadn't.

"I have a feeling you're going to get to know him real soon."

There was movement inside the fort. Some of the Argus robots, climbing carefully to the top of the wall, began to hand down the topmost prototypes; others were widening the opening at the wall's base. A stream of little robots started to carry devices out through the opening and off to either side of the fort, where they placed them several feet apart. As the opening in the wall grew larger Ben could see another group of Arguses doing the same thing at the fort's far wall. You could already see the lintel of the stairwell's door.

After a few moments the fort had been breached. The Containment Squad burst through the doorway and ran toward Ben and Rocklynne. Their hands were covered by heavy gloves, and face masks were dangling around their necks; they carried shielded tarpaulins, neutralizing gel, and expanding barriers. Four of them were towing floating pallets that were loaded with cannisters and spray equipment. "Where?" their leader barked, and Rocklynne pointed down the hallway.

"We should lead the Squad to the trouble site," he told Ben. "Don't you say another word to the Arguses."

Ben had been watching those little robots. Once they'd cleared the way for the Containment Squad they began to huddle together in little groups, facing inward. It looked like they were pretending that they were all alone on Level Eleven. Which was fair enough. They'd had a bad day, he knew.

Ben and Rocklynne left them behind and led the Containment Squad deeper into the level in the direction of the Low-Velocity Viscosity Projector and the Universal Electron Inverter.

Ben never felt at ease around the Containment Squad. Maybe it was their uniforms, and those goggled masks they

RATE

wore, but they all looked pretty much like the same person. The same tall, muscular, grim kind of person. Sometimes he wondered if they were all raised together on a secret island, somewhere.

He smiled at the squad leader. "What about those Arguses? Sensitive little fellas."

The squad leader – who was tall, and muscular, and grim – gave him a look. "You took the class, right?"

Ben pointed to the right. "Here we go. The problem is right down that aisle." He was awfully tired of hearing about that class.

"One thing," Rocklynne muttered. "When did we start giving tours to, you know, *students*?"

"You kidding?" Ben gave him a look. "Tours of the Registry? What kind of idiot would give tours of the Registry?"

He really hated being down in the Vault. It'd be a relief to get back to the office where he could have some of Violet's good coffee.

Ben couldn't take his eyes off the coffee pot. It was the same old pot: the one that Violet used to brew the best coffee in the building. But it didn't belong in *Ben's* office. It looked strange in here. It was just *wrong.*

"He *banished* the *percolator*?"

"He drinks tea. And he says he... he hates the smell of coffee."

It was just about unthinkable.

"Well, of course I don't mind. It's welcome in here. I just...."

He'd come upstairs hoping for a return to order, to the familiar rhythms of his life in the office, and what he'd found was chaos.

"I'll pop in a couple of times a day to make a pot," Violet said.

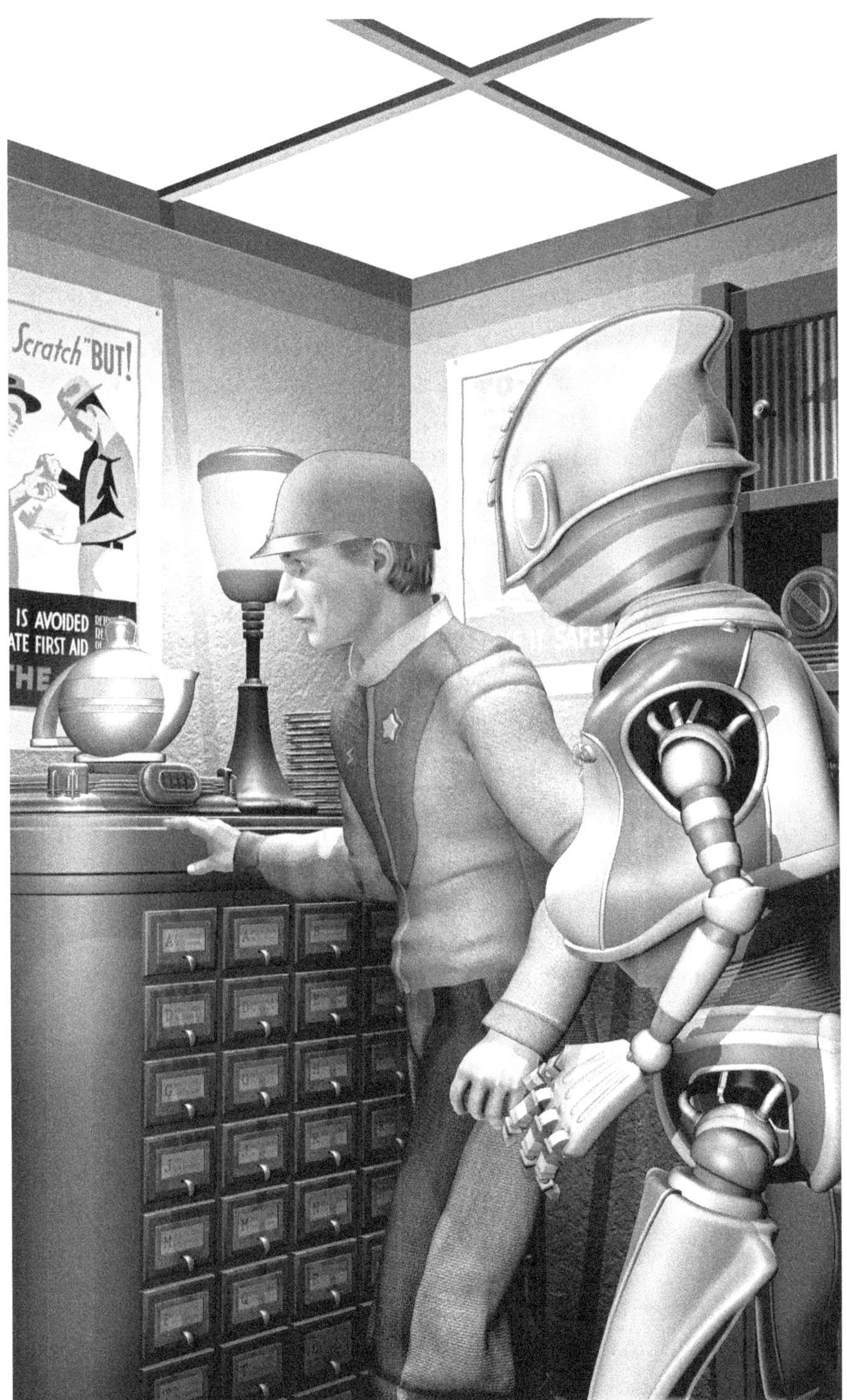
Scratch" BUT!
IS AVOIDED
FIRST AID

He nodded. That would be nice, anyway.

"You can't trust a man who hates coffee," he said. "It's not natural."

"You haven't even seen his mustache," Violet observed."It's like a caterpillar died on his face. But there's more than that. There's something very strange about this Registrar."

"Stranger than... that?" Ben was still staring at the percolator.

"He has this idea that civic organizations should be run for profit," she said. "He has a lot of ideas along those lines."

Ben tried to imagine how the Registry could be made commercial. He couldn't see a way.

"Why would you do that?" he asked. "What would we do with the money?"

"He's talked about buying more Info-Slates. But he has other ideas, too. He was very curious about the Containment Squad. He thinks it's wasteful to keep them on salary all the time, when we haven't needed them for two years. Until today, I mean."

"You don't need 'em often, but when you *do*...."

"Yes. You *really* need them when you need them. Registrar Cartier thinks they should be independent contractors. We would pay them just when we had to use them."

"That doesn't make sense either," Ben said. He didn't like the Containment Squad. They treated him like a... like a *human-person-who-has-not-yet-achieved-his-full-growth*. But there were a lot of things he didn't like that were still very important, no matter how he felt about them. "You'd get a whole different class of squad. Amateurs. The good ones would move on to where they could make a living."

"That's certainly one of the problems. Another is that we're *required* to staff the Squad, since we're storing all these dangerous devices outside the Experimental Research District. But the new Registrar doesn't seem very concerned about our legal responsibilities."

She pulled a can of coffee out of one of Ben's drawers and

started to brew a pot. Ben sighed.

"You know the Registry doesn't have any way to *handle* revenue, Ben? Even if we were able to generate an income... somehow... there's nothing we could do with it. Not legally. There's no place for it to *go*."

The first faint wisps of vapor started to rise from the coffee pot. "Where you're going with this," Ben said, "is that the Registrar is pretty well certain to break the law. One way or another. Or every which way, from the sound of it."

Violet nodded.

"And that being the case, well, somebody ought to sort of mount an investigation into him."

She nodded again.

"Which is what they call mutiny, I think."

"We're not on a ship, Ben. We're in a small and under-funded but vital branch of City Government. We're supervised by appointees who have no idea what we do or how we do it."

"It seems like this fella is figuring things out pretty quick."

"He's especially interested in what happens to the income from patents whose inventors have died," she said. "And when we came back to the office he asked me to requisition a typewriter. For *himself*. For what he called *confidential correspondence*. As if I...."

At this point Ben could have mentioned a few times when Violet's management of correspondence had been unusual, maybe even irregular. But the coffee was perking happily now, and as a stupidly smart person he decided to concentrate on that instead.

"Yeah, the way you put it, it does sound suspicious."

"Ben, I think you need to investigate the Registrar."

"No...." He thought carefully. This was going to be delicate. "I wouldn't feel right about running an investigation into my own boss. I mean, not without some kind of orders from over his head. No, a Patent Investigator is authorized to investigate patent registrations, and patent conflicts, and fishy business that comes out of the District. A criminal investigation, which is what you're talking about, that's like a whole different matter."

Violet pulled Ben's coffee cup out of another drawer. He was really going to have to look in those drawers some day. It seemed like there were all kinds of things in there he didn't know about.

She poured a cup of coffee and handed it to him. She didn't say anything, but Ben could see by her dimmed lenses and the slant of her shoulders that she was taking it pretty hard.

"Now, although I can't undertake an investigation such as you describe, I can see how I might *assist* in an investigation, you know, as needed. If there was a talented investigator with good instincts, somebody who is *not* a Patent Investigator, and isn't what you would call *precluded* from investigating the Registrar. As I am. If somebody *else* was investigating him I would see no barrier to assisting from time to time. As, like, a training exercise."

"I'm not an investigator, Ben. I told you. I'm a secretary. I'm not trying to get that promotion any more."

"Oh, but there ain't any promotion in it, is there? You investigate the boss, he's not very likely to give you a medal."

She looked at him. Her eyes weren't getting any brighter. Ben took a sip of that good, good coffee.

"Yep, I'd be more than happy to *assist* in an investigation like that. I just can't take the lead, is what I'm saying. For reasons of professionalism."

"You're trying to do a good thing here, Ben. I know you are. But it's the wrong thing. Every time I've tried to... to become an investigator, it's just hurt people all around me. I can't do it any more. You don't even *know* all the things I've...."

"Way I see it, Violet, that's the only way it's going to get done. It's got to be you."

He knew he had her. She just hadn't figured it out yet herself. But he could wait.

"This sure is good coffee," he said.

Violet looked at the coffee pot. It still seemed out of place in here: maybe she'd bring Ben a potted plant. Something resilient, because she knew Ben wasn't much good at nurturing. Which reminded her of something.

"Oh!" she said. "I made an appointment for you at the League of Robotic Persons. For your Argus class."

Everybody was after Ben to be more sensitive. He guessed he could handle it, if he had to.

"Sure, Violet. That'd be great."

They watched the coffee pot bubble, full of its delicious possibilities, while the normal bustle of the Registry office passed back and forth along the hall.

The Enigma of the Unseen Doctor

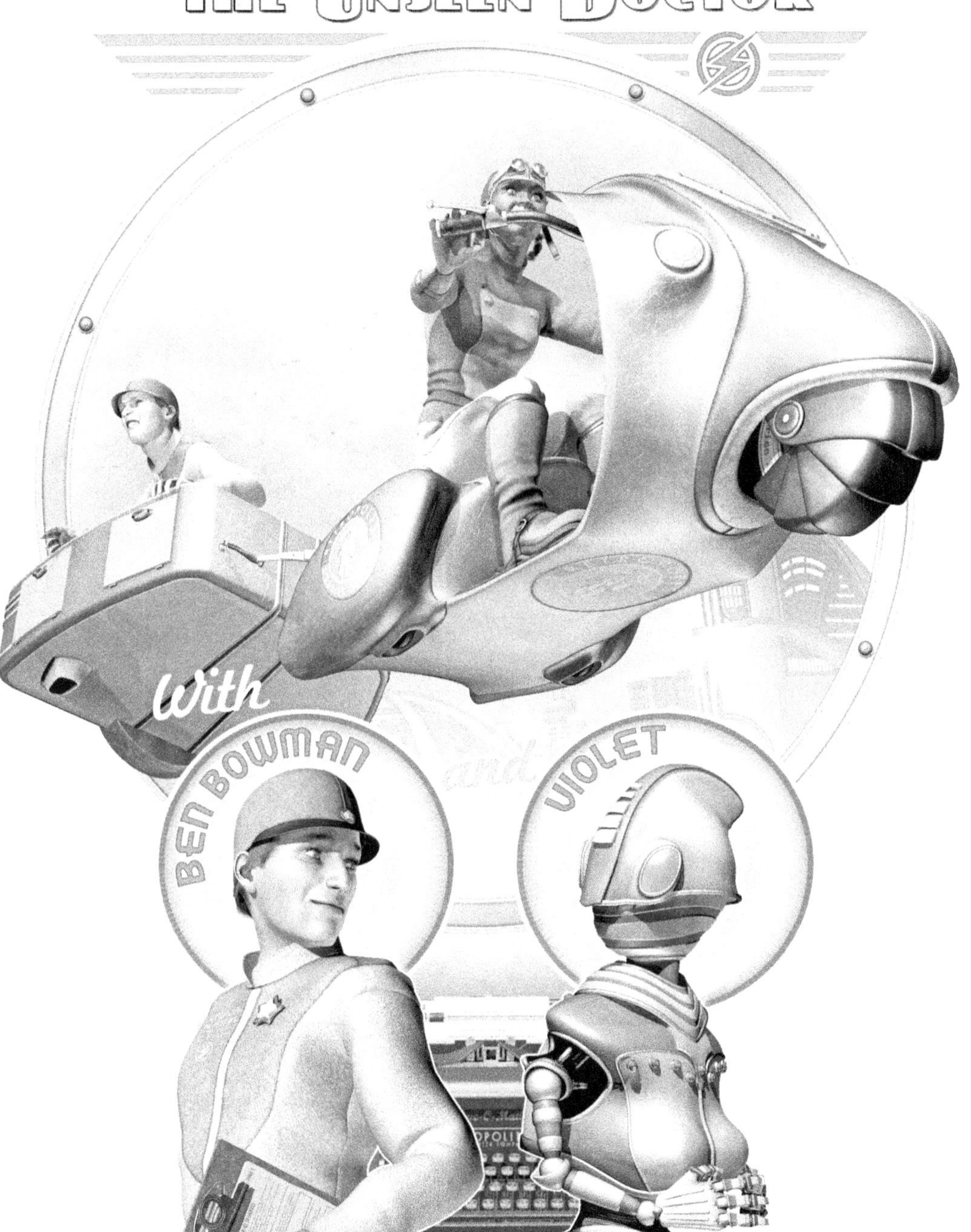

From the files of the Retropolis Registry of Patents

Ben had seen just about everything you could see in the Experimental Research District. He'd even seen things that you *couldn't* see. You saw them all the time. About a quarter mile from here he'd seen a large, orange crater, where the laboratory of Doctor Fenwick used to be, and that settled the question of whether Fenwick's research was as hazardous as it sounded. Another half mile toward the edge of the District was the site of Professor Haggard's laboratory; Ben planned to avoid that one on his trip back to the Registry of Patents, due to the contents of the preliminary patent application he'd picked up on his way in. It had described something that you would really rather *not* see.

These were the common, day-to-day details of a patent investigator's day. Ben hardly had to think about them any more.

And it wasn't unheard-of for an investigator to arrive at a laboratory's address only to discover that its owner, and the building, weren't located there today. But this?

Doctor Peregoy's laboratory was just where Ben had left it; but the plaque on the door now read "Doctor Sheckley". So, Ben figured, there were two possibilities. Either Doctor Peregoy had been meddling with the barriers between between parallel universes, in one of which her name was "Sheckley", or her experiments had turned out to be lethal in a very personal and localized way. It could be either one.

"She moved," said a voice behind him.

Ben jumped. You had to *always* be aware of what was behind you in his line of work, at least when that work had taken you into the District.

"It's all right," said the voice. "Courier Service."

The courier was bobbing up and down behind Ben, packages carefully arranged in the floating cart behind her floating scooter. "Didn't mean to startle you. But Doctor Peregoy, she's over on Insubstantial Avenue now. As of Tuesday."

Ben looked from her to the laboratory, then back again. "Moved?"

"Filed a change of address form. Aren't you Investigator Bowman? I'm Grace Keaton. I think we both know Violet."

Ben shook her hand, the one that wasn't holding a fat envelope. "Okay, Insubstantial Avenue. Strange – I don't think I've ever known one of the scientists to move before."

Grace fastened her scooter's straps to cleats set in the pavement. The scooter drifted a little in the breeze.

"She's three doors down from Euclid. There's a moat, you want to be careful of that one."

"An upgrade, then?"

Grace frowned. "I don't know. It's a lot smaller."

"But there's the moat."

"Yeah, like I said, watch yourself. Due to the biology."

Doctor Peregoy had a preference for biological experiments.

Grace lifted the envelope. "I should make my delivery. Say hello to Violet for me."

Ben watched her ascend the laboratory steps, being especially careful of the ninth one, and when she reached the top she slid the envelope into a slot in the door. He was still standing there when she came back down.

"Just paperwork today," he observed.

"That's all he (or she) ever seems to get. And send. Lots of papers. None of the hazardous materials, so far."

"An easy one," Ben said.

She unfastened her scooter and hopped on. "So far, sure. But you can't –"

"– make assumptions," he finished.

Grace nodded and for a moment their eyes met with that special understanding you always saw between people whose jobs took them to the District.

"Not my business," she said, "but you really should have known I was behind you." Then she took off toward her next delivery.

She was right about that. Ben didn't get sore about it. He'd just been kind of tired, lately, with training all the new investigators. And with the late nights in his studio at home.

He was going to have to cut back on those late nights. He knew he had to do that. But right now he needed to plot a route to the corner of Insubstantial and Euclid, so he could take care of this business and get out of the District alive.

Back at the office, Ben stopped at Violet's desk outside the Registrar's office. The Registrar's door was closed, and she was just sitting there with her chassis gleaming in the light from the lamp.

"Doctor Peregoy's address has changed," he said. "We need to update the records."

He waited for her to be surprised. But she simply nodded, her glowing lenses aimed at the Registrar's door.

"And I met Grace Keaton out there," he added. "She says hello."

He waited for a moment more. Then he went over to his office to make some coffee.

Violet really hadn't been herself, these past few weeks. In fact she hadn't been herself since the death of Registrar Sandrov. But this new Registrar had really gotten to her. Not in the usual way, like all the Registrars who had refused to promote her to investigator; but in a special, sinister way. She was convinced that he was up to no good.

Ben had tried to get her started on an investigation into

the Registrar. He wasn't sure how that was going, though, because Registrar Cartier had promoted half the patent officers to investigators. Ben, like every one of the old investigators, had his hands full helping the new ones along.

It's not that there was anything wrong with the new investigators. But any time you added a lot of new workers to a task you had to expect to lose some productivity before you could gain some. Never failed.

Ben slammed shut the fourth drawer in his cabinet and opened the fifth one. He never could remember where the coffee was stowed.

"Next to that one," he heard Violet say from the doorway. "Just like yesterday."

Ben stood aside and let her fill the pot. It was always better, for some reason, when Violet brewed it.

"Quiet day today?" he asked.

Violet slammed the lid on the coffee pot. "That man doesn't want a secretary," she said. "With all his *confidential typing*."

The office had grown accustomed to the slow, careful typing noises that came from behind the Registrar's closed door. There was a lot of backspacing; a lot of striking out. No one but Violet seemed to mind it. They were all happy about their newly issued Info-Slates. Some of them were so happy with the Slates that they weren't even carrying their clipboards any more.

Ben's eyes wandered to the empty hallway outside the door. He leaned in closer. "You learn anything new about him?"

Violet looked at the hallway, too. "I'm trying to locate his old secretary from the Zoning Registry. There's not a lot in the official records."

"You know if you need me, I'm happy to help," he told her.

They straightened when Investigator Bok poked her head in. "Ben, you got a minute? I think I have a Code Red."

They all thought they had Code Reds. This was the third one so far today.

"Come on in and tell me about it," he said, waving at his guest chair.

Violet pressed the button on the base of the coffee pot and left without another word.

He hated watching her go like that, but he didn't know what else to do. So he slumped into the chair behind his desk and smiled at Investigator Bok. "Okay," he said. "Let's hear about that Code Red."

Violet met Hazel on the steps of the Fraternal League of Robotic Persons. It was the end of Hazel's shift at the League counter, but the beginning of the busiest time of the day because of all the other robots who were ending their workdays around the city. Quite a few of them were coming to the League to drop off their dues, or to pick up their indenture claims, or to take care of some other business. So there was a tide of robots surging up the steps while Hazel and a few other clerks did their best to surge down.

As busy as it was, there was a hush over the crowd while they made their way up the stairs: an almost reverential hush. It was the way they all felt about the League.

Violet was carrying a neatly folded, brown envelope. Hazel pretended that she hadn't noticed it.

They made an odd pair. Violet had proportions that were, more or less, the proportions of a human person; Hazel's body was practically a sphere. People, whether human or mechanical, tended to get out of her way. That did make progress along the walkways a bit easier, even with the end-of-the-day rush going on, but Violet had always wondered how Hazel managed the narrow aisles of the monorails.Of course she'd never asked.

OWN and HENDERSON'S
ccessor to "Sunny Side Up"
B R E N D E L
Rocket
6.50
Shoes
FUN FOR THE WHOLE FAMILY!
TAKEN
INTERNALLY
SAFE
WHEN USED AS
DIRECTED

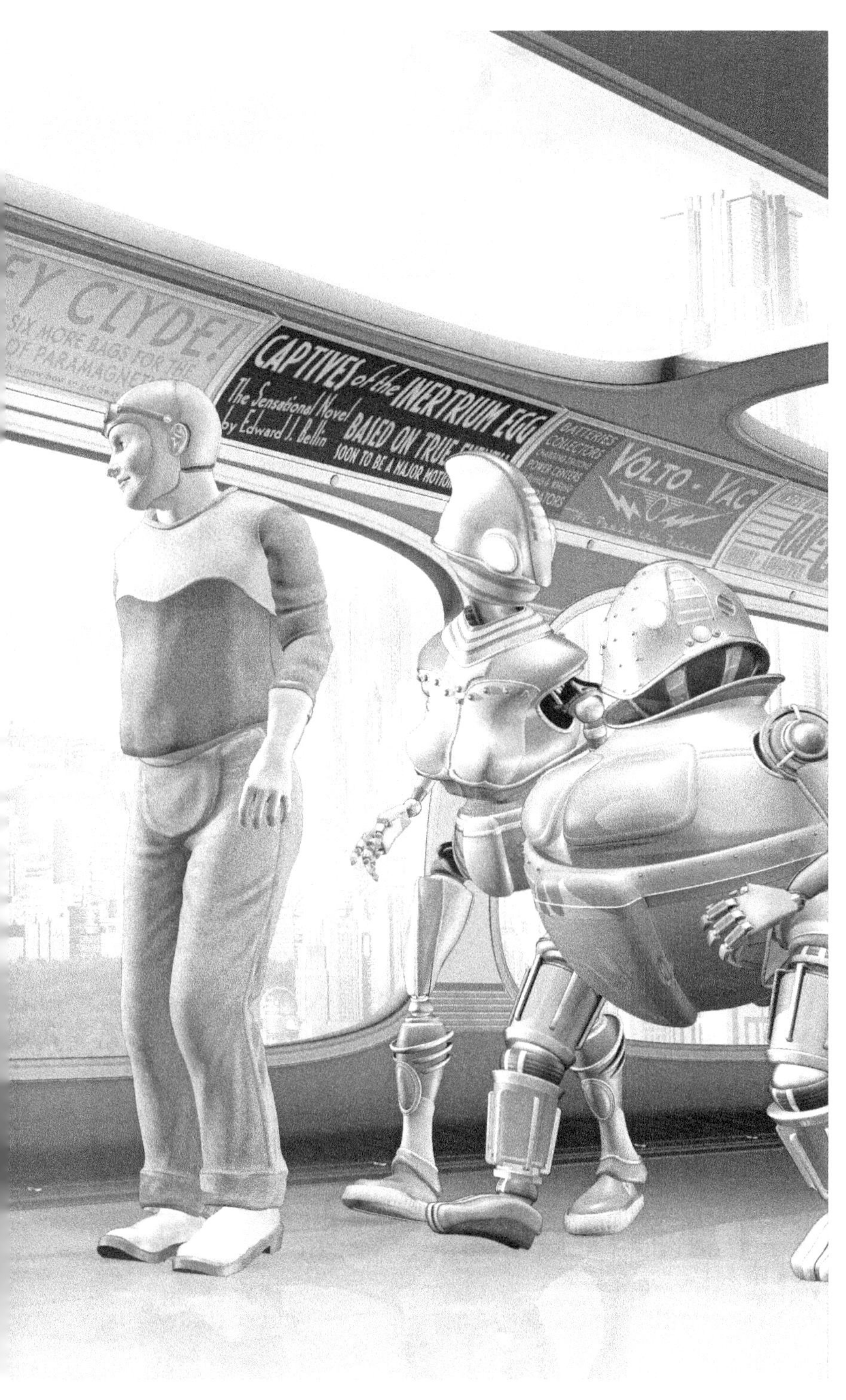
CLYDE!
SIX MORE BAGS FOR THE
CAPTIVES of the INERTRIUM EGG
The Sensational Novel
by Edward J. Bellin
SOON TO BE A MAJOR
BATTERIES
COLLECTORS
POWER CENTERS
VOLTO-VAC

Without even discussing it, the two of them wandered on up the nearby steps to the Constellation Skyway so that they could travel above ground level. The transparent skyway walls gave them a striking view over the tree-lined walkways of Retropolis, with far-off towers showing between the nearer ones in a vista that spread out into the haze of distance. They were close enough to the Green Line that most of the nearby buildings had left open corridors for the monorail tracks and, because the Northeast Orchard XXIV greenbelt was just a few blocks away, the landscape was as stunning as the architecture. This was their favorite walk in the vicinity of the League. And it was indirect, so they were able to leave the crowds below.

"So I looked into your problem," Hazel said at last. "I wish I had better news for you."

Hazel, like the other clerks, handled indenture payouts and dues collection at League headquarters. As a result she had access to information about every League robot in Retropolis, where almost every robot was a League member. So, if Registrar Cartier had a robot secretary in his time at the Zoning Registry, Hazel would know who that was.

"Nobody, then?"

Hazel's head swiveled back and forth. "He must have had a human secretary over there."

"Well, it was always possible. At least I know." Violet patted Hazel on the shoulder. "Thanks for looking."

Hazel's gaze drifted down to the envelope in Violet's hand. "There's... well, there's one thing. We *do* have a robot in the secretarial pool. But she's still indentured, so... well, you know how they are."

Violet didn't know how they were.

"Nervous, I mean. Won't want to make any trouble. Won't want to attract any attention. It's not like much can go wrong, but an indentured robot, she's usually terrified of losing her job."

Violet could see the sense of that. "Yes, I guess that's true.

She'd be afraid of being thrown into temporary jobs, or free-lancing."

"It could take so much longer, you know, to pay off the indenture. Without that steady paycheck. My advice, you meet her by accident, mention where you work, and, hey, you've got something in common. Like that."

Violet could see that Hazel's eyes were fixed on the envelope. She handed it to her, and Hazel gave Violet the name and address of the Zoning Registry secretary.

Hazel tore off the neat brown wrapping. Inside were the colorful covers of next month's *Hearts and Pistons* and *Throbbing Servos*, along with...

"*Turbines of Love #1!*" Hazel cried. "How did you *get* this one? It's not supposed to be out for *weeks!*"

"Anything for you, Hazel."

There was a well-established network of robot office workers, and Violet occupied a place near the center of its web. You just had to know the right people. The receptionist at Heart's Highroads Publications? She was one of those people.

She'd known that Hazel would be delighted, but seeing the spherical clerk's rapture was enough to make Violet wish that she could smile. She'd never tell Hazel what she'd had to arrange in order to get those advance issues. In fact, she'd never tell anybody. It was the kind of thing that made people wonder about you.

One half of Violet's success was that no one *ever* wondered about her.

They had a nice visit, walking along the Constellation Skyway, but Violet could see that Hazel was eager to get her treasures home. So before long she made an excuse and went home herself. She was going to have to think about this accidental meeting business.

It took more than a week, but Violet did her research and first happened to run into Agnes, a robot supervisor at Ray-O-Vac's Manufactory 114C. Agnes had come off the assembly line with Carmen, the Zoning Registry secretary. They'd stayed friends. After a couple of pleasant evenings out, Violet and Agnes went to the theater with Carmen and a few others.

Agnes had been good company, and would probably turn out to be a useful asset in the future. But once they'd enjoyed the show and stopped at a nightclub Violet was able to concentrate on Carmen, as she'd intended all along.

But, as Hazel had said, Carmen was a difficult problem. As soon as Violet mentioned the name of her new Registrar Carmen shuffled nervously and cut her off. "I don't know anything about that," she said. "I just do my job."

This did tell Violet that there was a "that", of course. "No, I understand," she said. She patted Carmen's aluminum forearm. "I was just thinking that his old secretary, there at the Zoning Registry... you know, I've forgotten her name. It was...."

"I don't know anything about her," Carmen said. "I just do my job."

"Very commendable." Violet let it rest for a few minutes.

They had a conversation about the play they'd just seen, and how very appealing the lead actor had been, with his wide steely shoulders and his smoldering glass eyes. The flared, streamlined vents on the rear of his pelvis had caught everyone's attention.

Violet commented on the wonderful sets. Such a nice apartment interior, so very restrained and attractive. So clean.

"Oh, don't get me started," said Carmen. "I'm stuck in this *terrible* apartment. It's hideous, and the pipes in the ceiling broke last month, and I can't get out of the lease for another *year.*"

"That's awful," Violet said. Then she had what seemed to be a sudden idea. "Say, I think I know somebody over at the

Housing Authority who might be able to help."

It only took a few more minutes.

The Registrar's secretary at the Zoning Registry had been Calliope Belbas, a human woman. She'd left her job shortly after Registrar Cartier took over at the Registry of Patents.

Carmen even knew her home address.

"But she wasn't there," Violet told Ben. "She moved out the same day that she quit her job at the Zoning Registry, and no one knows where she went. It's a dead end."

They were sitting in Ben's office. The door was closed. Ben was drinking some of that good coffee.

"But here's the thing," he said. "Now you know that something was going on over there, with your robot, that Carmen, all flustered when you asked about it. And this one, this Calliope, she just disappeared."

"It's 'Cal-ee-OH-pee'", she corrected him. "It's Greek."

"Right, CalleeOhpee, whatever, she just up and vanished on you. You *know* something peculiar was going on."

Violet nodded. "I'm looking into her background. It's about all I can do, for now."

Ben sipped his coffee. "Good work, though, finding all that out. Good investigatory work."

Violet didn't comment. She'd told him, over and over, that she wasn't angling for an investigator's job any more. But he didn't seem to take it in.

"Anything more from Carmen?" he asked.

"I don't think so. It wasn't easy, getting the name and address. She's too afraid of losing her job."

He sighed. Violet really wished she could do that: it was so versatile.

"You've got that meeting in a couple of minutes," she reminded him. "With the new investigators."

TO-DAY
IS ANOTHER DAY
RETROPOLIS
REGISTRY
OF PATENTS
RROP
RETROPOLIS
REGISTRY
OF PATENTS

RETROPOLIS
REGISTRY
OF PATENTS
SAUNDERS ROOM
CONFERENCE C

He sighed again.

"And I need to look over the day's assignments anyway," she added on her way to the door. "We just don't have enough officers, with all the promotions. You're all going to end up doing some officer work as well. Again."

She didn't wait for the third sigh. But she knew it was happening right behind her.

They did have *one* new officer, Officer Arriaga, and she was already there in the conference room when he arrived. Very studious, Arriaga, always making notes of everything he said. It was sort of flattering.

But Violet had been right about the workload. All these new investigators had been doing the small jobs before, when they were officers. And now there were plenty of investigators, but not enough officers to do those small jobs. So, every day, the investigators had to go through the District to collect forms: preliminary application forms, which were very important, and the final applications, and then when a patent was approved you had to hand-deliver the paperwork to the scientist who'd applied for it. It was a lot of footwork, and a lot of paperwork; and it barely left them enough time to conduct the investigations they were supposed to be doing all along.

"Now that we have all this help," he said, "we could really use some help with it."

The investigators and officers could see the humor in that, in spite of everything.

"Thing I don't get," he went on, "is how we're paying for it. All those new Info-Slates you're using, and the payroll for all the investigators, now, when we couldn't even stretch the budget at all a few weeks ago."

"It's not like we was costing them any more than we did when we was officers," somebody said.

Ben didn't see how that was possible, so he said "I don't see how that's possible. I mean, your base pay as an investigator, it's…." He remembered that there were officers in the room, and so he coughed. "… you know, it's, uh, it's *somewhat higher* than your pay as an officer."

"Not while we're on that Provisional Program," said Investigator Rocklynne. "Not until, what did he say, the *situation is resolved*."

"What situation?" Ben asked.

The new investigators looked at each other. "The thing with the…."

"You know, the fiduciary balance, and its, what do you call it?"

"The temporary emergency situation."

"The regrettable but inevitable something something."

They fell silent.

"So let me see," Ben said. "You're all investigators now, right? You've got the uniform, and the badge, and everything. But you're still making officer pay."

They agreed.

"And meanwhile, like, we're all still doing the officer jobs in addition to the investigator jobs. Am I right?"

They agreed with this, also.

"So nothing has actually changed."

There was a pause, while everyone tried to decide whether they went along with this one, too.

"You know," said Investigator Bok, "maybe we need a union."

There was another silence, so deep that Ben could hear the scratching sound of Officer Arriaga's pen.

"Well," said Investigator Fearn. "We've got the badges."

There was a murmur of assent.

"And we've got these new Info-Slates."

Everyone looked at their new Info-Slates, which were convenient, and very stylish, as well.

"And we're *all* doing two jobs now, for the same pay as

before," said Investigator Bok.

There wasn't much of a meeting after that. Oh, they went on for awhile. But a terrible comprehension had passed across the room and there didn't seem to be anything that could compete with it.

All but Officer Arriaga. She was still writing in her little notebook. But she was just an officer, so this didn't really apply to her.

Officer Bok didn't come in, next morning. Violet showed Ben the letter.

"Accumulated vacation days," he read. "Huh."

"What went on in that meeting yesterday?"

"Well, it was interesting,"

He told her about it. They were in his office again. The door was closed, again.

"I wonder how many vacation days *I* have?"

"Forty-three. You didn't take that fishing trip, you know, when...."

"Yeah. I know. You know what else I know? This letter is *typed*."

"Officer... I mean, Investigator Bok doesn't have a typewriter," Violet said.

"She could have used yours, I guess. You said the letter was on your desk this morning?"

Violet took the sheet back from him. "No, this wasn't typed on my typewriter. The typeface is different."

Ben was surprised to hear that type had a face, but he didn't mention it.

"What about the Registrar's typewriter? What kind of face does its type have?"

Violet set the letter down. "I don't know. I've never seen any of the documents he types in there."

"You know, I kind of hate it that I'm thinking about this,

but maybe we should find out."

"About his typeface."

"Yeah. About that."

The letter sat on Ben's desk in between them. They were both staring at it.

"Off– Investigator Bok, yesterday...."

"She said something about forming a union," Ben said. "And about our doing two jobs now for the same pay. But we were all talking about that."

"Everybody?"

"Just about everybody."

"But no one else was talking about a union," Violet concluded.

"Yeah. I mean, no, nobody else mentioned that."

Neither one of them wanted to touch the letter now. Not until they knew for certain. But Violet was going to have to put it in Investigator Bok's personnel file, so she picked it up by one corner.

"I'll find out about the typewriter," she said. "I'm not sure how; he keeps his door locked, and I don't have the key. But I'll find out."

Now that Investigator Bok had left, they had even fewer people to do the same work as before. So it was a pretty hectic day, and Ben knew it wasn't going to be the last one.

He was able to finish up the Doctor Peregoy investigation, and that was something. But there were a lot of pick-ups to do around the District, and when he found himself back on Doctor Peregoy's old street he started to wonder about that scientist in her former lab. Stuttley? Stuffley?

He walked over that way. Sheckley. Doctor Sheckley. After shuffling through his assignments, he started to wonder about Doctor Sheckley. He (or she) wasn't filing any preliminary applications – always a danger sign – although, according to

NON-LINEAR LIQUEFACTION
Do not forget the integer thing
CHART OF ELECTROMAGNETIC RADIATIONS

Grace Keaton, he (or she) wasn't getting any large packages of material, either. But none of the scientists just sat around. The guy (or gal) had to be working on *something*.

Ben looked hopelessly at the list of assignments he still had to finish today. But he decided to take the time to introduce himself to Doctor Sheckley anyhow.

He remembered to step right over that ninth step to the porch and then he rang the bell, over and over, and he waited for quite awhile. But Doctor Sheckley wasn't taking visitors. Ben knew there was a slight possibility that the doctor had gone out. But as possibilities go, that one was as slim as an earthworm's spine. Which is to say nonexistent.

The scientists really didn't *go* anywhere: they were exactly where they wanted to be. Oh, there was some kind of secret society thing they all belonged to, and if you're going to have a secret society then you really have to go to meetings. Some time. Maybe when the Moon is new. But on your average, everyday day – every day, that is, until their *last* day – each scientist was just about stapled to his (or her) workbench.

Could be, Doctor Sheckley was using some really *big* staples and he (or she) couldn't come to the door. Ben made a note to look into it.

Then he went out again to continue his rounds.

Back in the office, Investigator Rocklynne came to Ben with another Code Red.

"Sit down," Ben said, "and tell me about it."

Rocklynne told him about it.

"That's not a Code Red," Ben said with some patience that he didn't really have. "When you were an officer you'd have *known* that's not a Code Red."

Rocklynne looked confused.

"It's because of the responsibility," Ben explained. "When you were an officer, you could just refer these things to an investigator and you didn't have to worry about them any more. But now you can't do that, am I right? *You're* the investigator. It's your responsibility. So you guys, all of you new guys, you're getting way too excited about preliminary applications right now. Because if you don't catch a hot one, nobody else will."

Rocklynne didn't seem convinced.

"It's okay. It means you're taking it seriously. You'll get used to it.

"Now, your real Code Red, you know what it's like. A preliminary application comes in from a scientist who wants to patent a method for, say, breeding bacteria that feeds on inertrium. Who knows why, it's not like that's a thing that anybody would want. But he figures he can do it if he applies himself, and he just can't resist. Now, you know that if he pulls that off we're going to see every rocket ship and every skyscraper in Retropolis hitting the ground real quick, because that bacteria's going to get loose and start eating all the lighter-than-air inertrium structures it can find. Right. Everybody dies. That's a Code Red."

"Well, that's one you did stop, though, right?"

"Yeah. Professor Fenwick IXc. And it wasn't easy. Maybe you remember. I had to pull every trick in the book, first to distract him, which I am sad to say did not work, and then to get him fighting with another scientist, and then fighting with his whole street, until finally he disappeared in that big blue cloud. That was a bad one. But, you know, when you're facing a real Code Red you just don't give up until you've stopped it. You've got no choice."

"Well, yeah. I know."

"Of course you know. And it's scary as anything to think you might miss one. And, believe me, I would rather see a hundred false Code Reds than one *real* one. So don't stop. You're doing the right thing. It's just that before long you'll get your perspective back, and you'll see the difference again."

"Between the real ones and the false ones."

"Yeah, that's all."

It seemed like he was getting through. The last thing he wanted was for Rocklynne to relax. But he'd be happy when the false Code Reds died down a little.

"This one you've got? I wouldn't worry about doubling the size of the Sun. Because, first..." Ben held up one finger. "...I don't think it's possible to attract all the hydrogen in the solar system to the Sun. If the Sun's own gravity can't do it, I don't think that Professor Wilcox can either. If there was enough hydrogen in the neighborhood to make the Sun a bigger star, that would have happened already. And, second?" He held up another finger. "The Sun eats hydrogen for lunch. And it loves it. You give it more, it'll burn hydrogen hotter. Longer. Not bigger. That's all."

"But..." Investigator Rocklynne wasn't quite ready to give it up. "If it was *enough* new hydrogen...."

"Not in this neighborhood, pal. If it wanted to be a bigger star, it should have set up shop someplace else."

"If you say so, Ben."

"You'd need to get a lot of hydrogen from *elsewhere*, which is an interesting problem," Ben continued. "Say you could gather all the hydrogen from six or seven nearby star systems, maybe by –"

He stopped himself in time.

"But not around here. Would not happen."

Rocklynne nodded. "Okay. But next time...."

"Oh, like I said, keep 'em coming. Plenty of false alarms, please. Those are the ones we want."

Rocklynne stood up and headed for Ben's door.

"Say, wait–" Ben said.

"Yeah?"

"You ever meet that Doctor Sheckley, in Doctor Peregoy's old laboratory? Doctor Sheckley doesn't seem to have filed any preliminaries at all, since moving in."

"Never heard of a Doctor Sheckley, Ben. Don't know that one at all."

“Yeah, okay. I’ll look it up. It’s just, with no preliminaries...”

“Yeah, you wonder what’s going on in there. Could be a....”

He smiled. “Just kidding, Ben.” And he walked out.

But he wasn’t wrong, Ben knew. If a scientist wasn’t filing any preliminary applications, there was no way to know what was going on in the lab. No way to know whether it was something that ought to be stopped.

Yeah, he was going to have to look into this Doctor Sheckley. He’d ask Violet to go through the files, see what they had. She could use a distraction.

But that only reminded him about Investigator Bok. And once he’d thought about her, it was hard to set it aside.

And he’d nearly lost control, talking to Rocklynne about the hydrogen. He could tell that it was going to be another long night in his studio. It’d be nice to get a good night’s sleep again, sometime soon. But he knew where he’d be tonight.

He just needed the release, that was all. He could stop any time he wanted.

Any time but tonight.

“No, Violet said. “It has to be tonight.”

The robot locksmith looked uncomfortable, which is a thing that a robot has to really work at.

It had taken days for Violet to mine all her city-wide connections to find a locksmith who belonged to the network. It had taken two more days to work out what that robot needed, and to find a way to get it. She was starting to feel the pressure. If Investigator Bok really was in trouble, Violet couldn’t wait any longer. And, anyway, she had to get into the Registrar’s office at night, when no one else was in the building. It had to be tonight.

“It’s my mother,” said the other robot. “If I’m not there for dinner, she’ll just be impossible.”

SPEEDY
KEYS
PRECISE
MADE WHILE U WAIT
DOOR CHECKS & FLOOR CHECKS
REPAIRED
HOME VISITS EXTRA
WHILE U WAIT

Violet tried to understand those two sentences. She tried again. Then she understood.

"You're in one of those trial family units?"

The locksmith nodded. "It seemed like a good idea. I'm not so sure, any more. My mother, she... she takes it very seriously."

Some robots had been experimenting with social units that corresponded to human families. The biggest difference, in Violet's view, was that these were arrangements that people entered into as a conscious choice; the groups couldn't help but differ from human families, in which everything happened, as it were, by accident. It would be reasonable to expect that the robot families would be more successful. Strangely, though, the results seemed to be mixed.

The locksmith was staring at his shop floor. Tiny highlights sparkled all around him, where keys and key blanks were still turning quietly on their hooks in the backwash from Violet's gestures.

"I tried to resign," he explained. "I'd had enough. But she got so, so... anyway, I can't be late for a family dinner. Not again."

"What are you having?"

He looked up. "Duckworth's Oil of Ilium."

Violet was impressed. "That's very good," she said. "It's so unusual to find Duckworth's these days. I used to use their three-weight lubricant all the time, back when you saw it everywhere. But here's what we can do: you have your dinner, and make peace with your family, and then we'll go to the Registry later. Maybe around eleven o'clock?"

"Oh, yes! That would be better. That would be much better."

It had to be tonight. But Violet could be flexible about exactly when.

"Say," said the locksmith. "Would you like to come to dinner with me?"

"I have another engagement," she said, with a simulation

of regret. There was no way she was going to be drawn into the locksmith's family drama. Not even for Duckworth's.

Violet arrived early, as she usually did, and as she lurked in the shadow of the trees at the Registry's north entrance she found herself imagining terrible situations for Investigator Bok. It wasn't productive.

So she was relieved to see the highlights of the locksmith's head appear in a pool of light far down the path. He vanished again as he passed out of the streetlight, then showed up again and again as he made his way along the path and in between the trees until at last he reached her. He seemed to be content. He was carrying a bag of tools.

"Dinner went well?" she asked.

"Yes, very well. They've settled down a bit."

Violet unlocked the side door to the office and led him into the dark, silent building. Although she knew it was best to stay out of this she couldn't help but ask. "They've... settled down?"

"Ever since I paid off my indenture to Mr. Nakamura I've been continuing to pay him. To buy the business from him, you know. He's grown quite old and infirm, the way they do."

Violet led the locksmith through the corridors, lit only by the softly glowing lamps of their mechanical eyes.

"I've known some robots who began to show their age," she observed. "It's not so different, until they get the refits."

"Poor Mr. Nakamura, though, he doesn't have a lot of refits available. So he's retired."

"Well, it sounds like a good arrangement for you both."

"Oh, it is! But my family wanted to help with the payments, you see. So I could own the whole shop sooner."

They passed the elevator banks; the three public elevators were on their left, and the one restricted elevator on their right. It led down to the Vault levels.

Violet could do this interpersonal arithmetic in, metaphorically speaking, her sleep. "And you're not sure you want your family to be your business partners."

The locksmith's eye lamps bobbed up and down. "It's one thing to *have* a family. It's another thing to have them involved in every part of your life."

"Yes, that could get complicated."

She unlocked the door to the little office where she spent her days, and turned on the lights. She pointed at the Registrar's door. "That's the one."

She thought about the locksmith's family while he crouched down by the door, opening his bag and sorting through his tools.

She'd never considered joining a family, but in some way perhaps her covert robot network was like one; in the practical aspects, anyway. Come to think of it, there were also dinners. But when you exchanged favors and information the boundaries were obvious, even when they weren't stated. It was more like a business transaction. She supposed that the unstructured connections of a family might have advantages, but as in any group of people– whether they were human or mechanical people–there would be a hierarchy, with the dominant personalities at the top. On the whole, she liked her way better.

The fact that she'd have been at the top didn't make the arrangement sound any more satisfactory, to Violet. She preferred to rule in a much less visible way.

"That's it," said the locksmith. The Registrar's door swung open.

Violet picked up a blank sheet of paper from her desk. "It'll just lock itself when I close it?"

"No, I'll need to do that from out here."

"This will just take a moment, then."

She stepped into the Registrar's office and over to his desk, where she pulled the cover from his typewriter. With unconscious grace she rolled the paper onto the platen and typed the few sentences of Investigator Bok's letter. Then she rolled the paper out and looked over her work.

She'd want to compare them, but the typed lines appeared to be identical. So she folded the paper and stowed it in a compartment just above her waistline. The cover went back over the typewriter, and she stepped back out into her own office. "All done."

The locksmith shook his head and locked the door again. "Well, I hope you got what you needed."

She assured him that she had, and turned off the lights as they went back out into the hall.

"I won't ask what it's about, of course," he said. "I'm just happy that I could help."

"I'll do my part tomorrow," she promised.

They went back out the way they'd come in, with their eye lamps again the only lights in the hall.

But just as they were about to turn off the main hall Violet was sure she heard something; a soft, brushing sound, like the noise of a sliding door. She took the locksmith by the arm and they stood quietly for a moment. There was no further sound.

"Did you hear that?" she asked.

"Something. Maybe. I thought I heard something."

Violet looked over the banks of elevator doors. None of the indicators were lit. None of the elevators were moving.

"Probably nothing," she murmured. "Probably nothing."

It was almost certainly nothing.

"There's probably nothing to it," Investigator Rocklynne was saying. He and Investigator Fearn were standing close together in the Registry hallway. "I just think we should look into it, is all."

Investigator Fearn nodded, first in agreement and then, to Violet, in greeting. "'Morning, Violet."

"Have you seen Ben?" she asked them.

"He went out early." Rocklynne told her. "Something he wanted to check."

Her copy of Investigator Bok's letter was still folded in Violet's hidden compartment, and she wanted to compare it to the original in the files. So she didn't ask them what it was they were going to look into. She just said, "You know if you need my help with anything..."

But they seemed to prefer to keep the matter, whatever it was, to themselves.

Violet hadn't even made it to the files when Registrar Cartier popped out of his office to say hello. This was unusual. He'd been quite talkative when he first started his job, but lately he'd withdrawn into his office and he'd had very little to say to his secretary.

"Everything going well, Violet?"

It took every electron of her willpower to keep her eyes

from focusing on his mustache.

Facial hair was rare among the human men of Retropolis. She'd seen it, but usually at a distance. And she understood that she was having a typical robot reaction to his mustache. It was not actually a rodent, crouching on his lip. It wasn't even much *like* a rodent, crouching on his lip. It just seemed completely out of place on a person's head.

It was as though she was trying to talk to a robot who had a big, rusty patch in the middle of his face. With wires springing out of it.

Why don't eyebrows bother me? She wondered. But things were as they were. So she kept her eyes aimed at his eyes, about three inches above the lurking creature near his mouth.

"About the same, Registrar," she said. "I've had a lot of time to work on the files lately."

Because you insist on doing all your own typing.

"You know, of course, that if you're worried about anything you can bring it to me," he said. His eyes were aimed just as precisely at hers. "*My door is always open.*"

Violet was often happy that her face was immobile. Robots didn't have the same involuntary expressions that humans did, and very few humans could read a robot's body language. So it was a simple matter for her to bob her expressionless head and murmur, "Yes, Registrar, I appreciate that."

"I've been meaning to speak to the staff about their Info-Slates," he went on. "Do they have a meeting today?"

"No, sir, there's one tomorrow afternoon. Is there a problem with the Slates?"

"Oh, no. No problem. It's just that if they're happy with their Info-Slates I think they might start talking about them. You know, when they're out on their rounds. And at home. And out with their friends. 'I can't believe I ever got along without one of these', and 'that's so much easier to do, now that I have this handy Info-Slate.' That sort of thing."

Violet though about it.

"Like an endorsement, you mean?"

"No, certainly not. Not an *endorsement*. As civil servants we can't make endorsements. No, I'm thinking more along the lines of a spontaneous recommendation. An exclamation, you know, just getting carried away by the sheer utility of the device. That sort of thing. Exuberant. Thrilled to have one. Overwhelmed by how useful it's turned out to be."

"Yes, sir. Well, as I said, the officers and investigators have a meeting tomorrow afternoon. Perhaps you could explain it to them then."

"Excellent!" The Registrar looked thrilled, possibly even exuberant. "I'll leave it to you, then, to add me to their agenda."

And with that the Registrar took himself, and *his* agenda, back into his office. Violet heard the key snick in the lock.

The shipment of Info-Slates had come directly from their manufacturer, Volto-Vac Industries. Violet searched through the files and found the invoice.

The return address was the marketing department.

So, she thought. *That's how we got all these Info-Slates without paying for them.*

She turned to Investigator Bok's personnel file and compared her letter to the one that Violet had typed last night on the Registrar's typewriter. They looked identical. She slipped the file back into its drawer and sat down at her desk. Where was Ben? She really wanted to tell him about this.

Ben was paying another visit to Doctor Peregoy. Their official business had been resolved, but there was something else he wanted to know.

"No," the doctor told him. "I never met Doctor Sheckley in person. He (or she) made the offer for my old laboratory through an intermediary. A Miss Harmonica Something. Or Harmonium. Something like that. A musical name."

Doctor Peregroy had accepted the offer–which was generous–and moved her lab into this much smaller building because she wanted to spend the rest of the money on the big, bubbling machine that she was now staring at. She seemed to be in love.

The Maritime High-Pressure Environment Simulator was a beast of a machine, and it filled this room from wall to wall. Ben couldn't imagine how it had been installed in here. You'd have to assemble it in place.

But it was just the thing to have if you wanted to keep a giant squid happy, and even though he had no way to ask the giant squid that was slowly moving around in there, it looked just about as happy as any giant squid that Ben had ever seen: and he'd seen a few, in his time.

Ben frowned. "A musical name...? Could it have been Calliope? Calliope Belbas?"

"It's on the paperwork," Doctor Peregroy said, She waved over at a cabinet in the hallway outside. She looked about as happy as a giant squid in a Maritime High-Pressure Environment Simulator.

So Ben walked over to the cabinet and shuffled through its papers, which were mainly patent registrations and royalty statements from the legal firm that handled licensing for Doctor Peregroy's patents. Eventually he found the sales contract.

It was signed by Calliope Belbas, for the Technological Investment and Benevolent Licensing Company. Ben had never heard of them. But he had heard of Calliope Belbas, who had been Registrar Cartier's secretary over at the Zoning Registry. And who had since disappeared.

Ben had a feeling that the Technological Investment and Benevolent Licensing Company would turn out to be owned by another company he'd never heard of, and that *that* company would just be the next stop on a long, convoluted chain of ownership that a team of accountants could unravel only after weeks of hacking their way through the corporate underbrush. In the end, he was sure that it would lead to Registrar Cartier. But why?

And who was Doctor Sheckley?

When he left Doctor Peregroy, happy with her happy squid, Ben could see that he was late for the office. But in spite of that he took a detour so that he could go by Doctor Sheckley's lab. There he found Grace Keaton once again tethering her scooter to the pavement. He walked right up to her so he could see the return address on the large envelope she was carrying.

Without turning around, she said "Good morning, Investigator." Show-off.

He looked down at the return address. "Well, that settles that," he said. "Doctor Sheckley must be a man."

"Couldn't say," said Miss Keaton. She thumbed up the bill of her cap. "Never met him (or her). Why do you think so?"

Ben pointed at the envelope. "I don't think any woman is likely to get mail from a prostate lawyer."

Miss Keaton went still. Very still. "A what?"

"A prostate lawyer."

"Probate," she said, very quietly. "A probate lawyer. That's a lawyer who handles wills, inheritances, that sort of thing."

Her face was still frozen when Ben took his leave. But he could have sworn she was laughing at him all the same. It could be that his preoccupation with her was one of the reasons for what happened next.

When Ben hadn't come back by noon, Violet began to get nervous; and her nervousness only increased as the hours dragged on and there was still no sign of him.

Even if Registrar Cartier was aware that Violet had broken into his office–and there wasn't much doubt as to that–he might not know what she'd done in there; and she had no reason to think that the Registrar would know enough to suspect Ben. But the continued absence of Investigator Bok was still weighing on Violet, and if Ben had disappeared now, too....

No one else had seen him. He hadn't ever arrived at the office. Whenever an officer or investigator returned from the District, Violet took them aside to ask. But there wasn't any sign of Ben.

The only other people missing were Investigators Rocklynne and Fearn. They were likely still engaged in whatever business had so absorbed them in the morning.

The hours went by. At last it was closing time, and Violet lingered for awhile even then. She'd tried calling Ben at home, but she got no answer. Finally she had no choice. She covered her typewriter, locked the door, and left the building.

Three blocks down the road she noticed Officer Arriaga a little way behind her. Arriaga was out of uniform. She must have changed before she left the building, which was unusual. Most of the officers and investigators wore their uniforms in

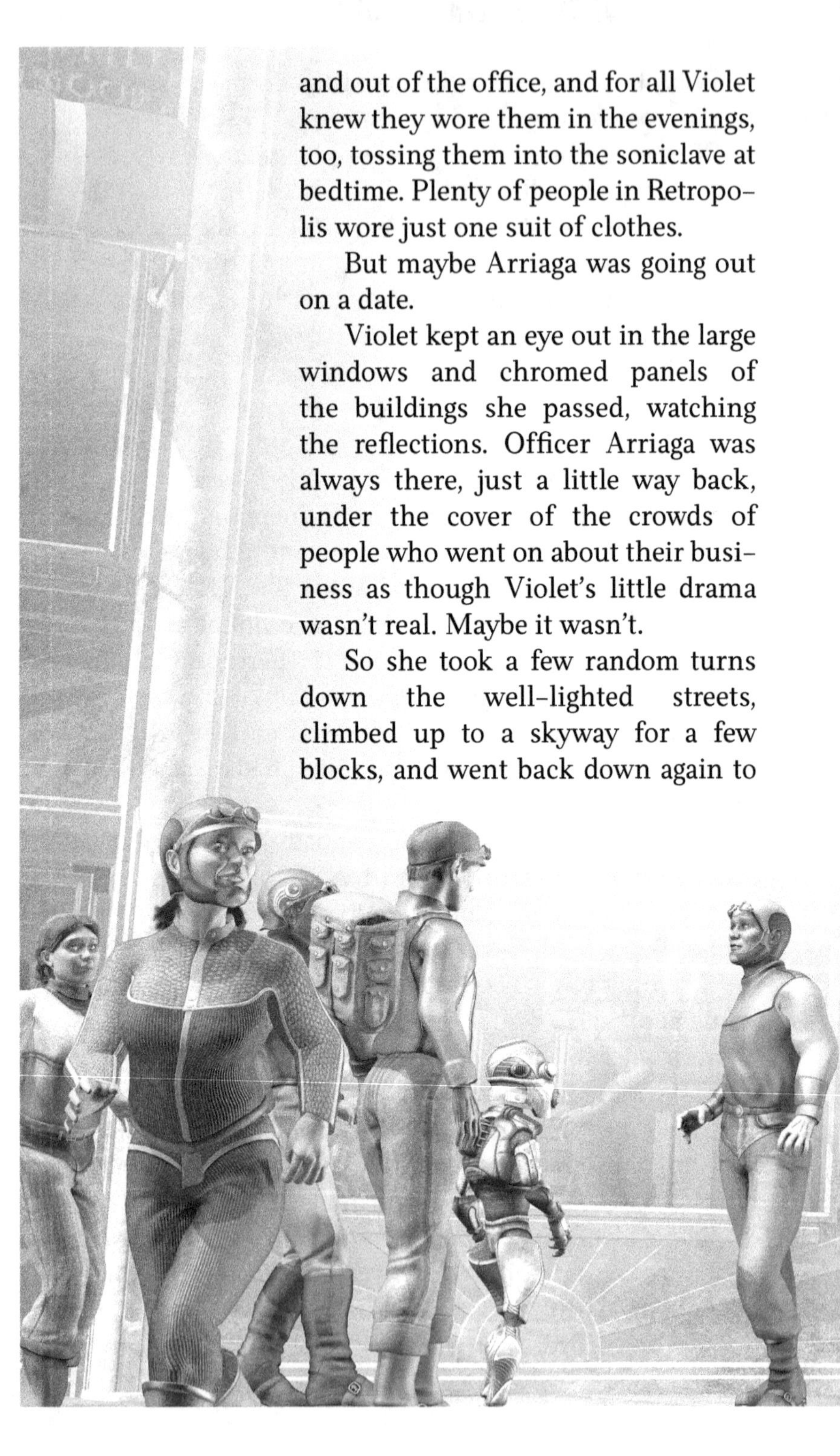

and out of the office, and for all Violet knew they wore them in the evenings, too, tossing them into the soniclave at bedtime. Plenty of people in Retropolis wore just one suit of clothes.

But maybe Arriaga was going out on a date.

Violet kept an eye out in the large windows and chromed panels of the buildings she passed, watching the reflections. Officer Arriaga was always there, just a little way back, under the cover of the crowds of people who went on about their business as though Violet's little drama wasn't real. Maybe it wasn't.

So she took a few random turns down the well-lighted streets, climbed up to a skyway for a few blocks, and went back down again to ground level. Officer Arriaga continued to keep her in sight.

This settled things, for Violet, and in more than one way. She didn't feel nervous any more: now she knew that something was going on, even if she wasn't sure what that was. If this was what had happened to Investigator Bok, then Violet would be careful to stay in crowds of people: until she didn't want crowds, anyway. And she knew exactly what crowd she wanted.

So she continued on her apparently aimless way for about two miles until it led her right up the steps of the Fraternal League of Robotic Persons.

This was a place where she could really melt into the crowd. Officer Arriaga, of course, would be more conspicuous here.

Violet lingered in one of the long lines at the counter. The officer didn't follow her in. So after a few minutes she left the line and went upstairs to a line of public televideo sets.

This time, after a pause, Ben answered.

"Violet?"

She saw him turn, as though he'd heard something. But all she saw behind him was a closed door. He turned back to face the televideo camera.

He didn't look well: he looked exhausted, really. He'd looked that way for several weeks now.

"Ben, I know how this sounds. But I'm being followed. It's Officer Arriaga. I've lost her, for the moment, but she must know where I live."

The lines in Ben's face went deeper, the way they do in human faces, and after one more look behind him he said, "Can you lose her for good? If you can, come here. If you can't–"

"No, I can. I'll be right over, Ben. And thank you."

"Not a problem, Violet. If you think she's on to you again, I'll come down myself."

And he would, she knew. She could always count on Ben. If he was only smart in a couple of the important ways, well, that still put him ahead of most persons. Violet knew that you're lucky in life to be smart in any way at all.

There are several side and back entrances to the League building: far too many for one person to keep them all in view. So Violet picked one with care, scouted the walkway outside, and slipped away.

She saw no sign of Officer Arriaga on her way to Ben's apartment.

She'd never been there before, though she naturally knew where Ben lived. His building was one of the bigger towers here, near the center of the Concentric Gardens district, and he lived on the fifty-third floor on the side that faced outward, toward the district's greenbelt. The view was lovely, just now, in the soft light of the evening, with the lights of the towers glowing orange in the gloom.

He came right to the door when she knocked, and he let her in quickly with a look down the hall. "You lost her?" he asked.

She had.

"Then tell me all about it."

She did.

"But I can't say for sure," she concluded, "that she's working with the Registrar. I think she is; I had this conviction that she'd followed Investigator Bok just as she was following me. But I've had time to think about it. There could be another explanation."

"She could be investigating the Registrar, just like you are," Ben agreed. This was one of the ways in which Ben was smart. "She might have been doing that since his days at the Zoning Registry."

"If she's the same person as Calliope Belbas," Violet said.

"Yeah, but that gets complicated too," Ben said, and he told her about his conversation with Doctor Peregoy. "If Arriaga *is* Calliope Belbas, then it's a pretty sure bet that she's doing something strange with that Doctor Sheckley. I don't think we can trust her either way."

Then he remembered something else, and after a moment of mental lexicology he explained that Doctor Sheckley was getting correspondence from a probate attorney. Something about an inheritance.

"Then maybe Sheckley has a history we can trace," said Violet. "He (or she) must be in somebody's court records, somewhere."

"Yeah, tomorrow. But I'm thinking you may need to stay out of sight. You know the Registrar's on to you—"

"I *think* the Registrar is on to me."

"–right, and you know that Officer Arriaga, whoever she is, is following you. People are just way too interested in you right now. It's a good time to disappear."

She thought about that. "Investigator Bok disappeared."

Ben thought about it, too. "It would be *nice* if she'd disappeared on purpose. But then there's the letter that Registrar Cartier forged."

They thought about it some more, but they just didn't have enough information to know. So at last Ben pointed at the open door, the one that led to his bedroom. "You can bunk in there for the night. I'll take the couch."

But that was ridiculous, and she told him so. Violet didn't need to sleep in a bed. "But what about..."

She was looking at the second door: the one that had been closed, when she'd called, and was still closed now.

"That's, uh, that's just storage," Ben said. "Pretty messy in there. I wouldn't want to put you in that room."

And that was fine, except that he was lying to her. Maybe that was also fine. There was no reason he had to tell her everything. But it did seem strange.

"What about you, though?" she asked. "You never came into the office at all. And you talked to Doctor Peregoy in the morning, and then Grace Keaton, but that was still early."

Ben sank into the couch. "Yeah, that. Take a seat, Violet. I had a heck of a day out there."

Ben had been distracted as he walked away from Doctor Sheckley's laboratory. He didn't explain why he was distracted; he just mentioned it, with the shame that an investigator ought to feel about that kind of oversight during his rounds in the District.

There were several things he failed to notice.

He had no idea, for example, that Investigators Fearn and Rocklynne were waving at him from the other end of the block. He didn't take in the fact that–although foot traffic in the District was often sparse–there was no one else in view. The closed, locked, barricaded laboratories looked down on either side. But no one was looking back.

And then, crucially, he didn't notice that a large circular hole had appeared in the pavement, right in front of him.

He only realized it was there once he was looking up at it from below.

The hole was remarkable. About eight feet in diameter, it formed a perfect circle that was ringed by orange sparks and roiling red smoke. But there was something odd about the sparks and the smoke. They didn't arc out and billow in three dimensions: they didn't seem to have any depth at all. They were like the swirls of paint you'd see just after a glass plate had slammed down and pressed them into position. Except that they were still sparking, and still billowing, and there wasn't a glass plate in the roof of the world.

Which was crystalline.

Now, Ben wasn't really able to take all of that in before he crashed into the ground below, because he didn't fall that far: just twelve or fifteen feet. But he landed on his back, so he was still looking up while he tried to make his lungs breathe again. And since that took more than one try he'd got a pretty good look at the hole, and the sparkling sky, by the time he was sure where he wasn't. Which was anyplace that he'd ever seen before.

The sky he could still see *through* the hole looked familiar, but it was moving, as though the world was spinning around up there. He saw bits of the scientists' laboratories, and the faraway clouds, and the occasional fraction of a fire escape. But the view was sweeping around in a plunging arc that made him feel a little bit sick, just looking at it. So he decided to look someplace else.

There was an awful lot of someplace else. And yet almost all of it looked about the same. Everything he could see was studded with crystals, and although the crystals came in all

sizes they each jutted outward, either from the ground, or from the roof–if that *was* a roof–like stalactites and stalagmites and any other kind of mite you could think of. The crystal spikes were translucent. A soft light glowed near the heart of each one.

And they went on for as far as Ben could see.

The only items in view that were not crystals were a human foot, about ten feet to Ben's left, and the roughly two-thirds of Professor Kline which had broken Ben's fall. Professor Kline had never liked Ben much, back in Ben's years at the Academy for the Unusually Inventive: the professor was always after him to *apply himself.*

Ben and the remains of the professor were in the middle of a circle of light that fell through the hole above. Beyond that circle it was only the glowing crystals that lit the endless landscape of the... cavern?

"HELLLLLLLOOOOOO", Ben called, and after a moment he heard a distant echo. "IS ANYBODY HERE?"

He waited. The reply, when he heard it, was very distant and indistinct. It might have been the sound of an avalanche, or the sound of far-off falling crystals. But it really sounded more like a roar. Like a big, long, angry roar.

Ben looked back up at the hole, and the sky beyond it. Not more than fifteen feet, he figured. The roar echoed again. It probably only sounded like it was closer.

The biggest crystal under the hole was about five or six feet tall. It wasn't really high enough, but he tried it anyway, jumping straight up from its tip. His fingers didn't even come close to the hole's edge. Did it even *have* an edge, something you could grab on to?

Ben heard the roar again. Yep, definitely closer this time. He climbed back down, avoiding the remnants of Professor Kline, and tried to pry another large crystal out of the ground. It felt like it had roots.

Something about the light changed. Ben looked up and saw that the sky above wasn't spinning any more. Rocklynne's face peered over the hole's edge. "Investigator Bowman? Ben? You all right in there?"

"Peachy," he answered. It was good to see Rocklynne. There was another roar, quite a bit closer this time.

"What was that?" Rocklynne asked.

"Let's not find out, okay? You have any ideas up there?"

"Fearn's bringing a–here she is. Hang on."

Ben watched them lower a ladder through the hole. It was long enough that it reached the ground.

"You need to get up here right away," Fearn said. She looked frightened, which was nice of her. "This thing only stays still for 2.43 minutes."

Ben swarmed up the ladder in much less time than that. At the level of the hole he looked out in the direction of all that roaring, and he was pretty sure he saw something moving out there in the distance: it was glowing green, in contrast to the soft blue light of the crystals.

He leaped from the ladder's top and landed on the pavement. The other two hauled the ladder up and threw it off to the side, just under a fire escape that was missing a ladder. Rocklynne pulled Ben back. "It's going to start moving again," he explained. "Right about–"

The circular hole didn't accelerate: one moment, it was stationary; the next, it had spun twelve feet away, and it kept going. Ben saw that he'd been standing right in its path.

When the hole spun outward and–somehow–directly under a laboratory, Ben said, "Okay. You'd better tell me what's going on."

"That almost sounds like a Code Red," Violet said. She was leaning back on Ben's couch. It was more comfortable than you'd think.

"It *is* a Code Red," he told her. "The hole's moving in a

spiral that grows about thirty feet per day. Its diameter is increasing by about a four inches per day. You don't really need to do the math: that thing's going to turn into a hole that swallows everything at ground level. When an important part of a building falls through..."

He didn't even finish. The conclusion was that obvious.

"Where... where does it go? Where were you?" Violet wondered.

"Someplace we don't want to be."

They sat in silence for a minute or so.

"Are they taking care of it?"

"Yeah, good marks for the team. But it's a tough one. Doctor de Camp couldn't be distracted; they tried using a forged preliminary application, you know, to make it look like someone else was working on the idea; then they got his neighbors all riled up, but nothing even slowed him down. They cut off power to his laboratory–"

"But de Camp's Patent #562997–"

"Yeah, the Persistent Air Ionizing Power Generator. As long as he has atmosphere, he's got power."

There was another brief silence.

"But they're–"

"Yeah, they're on top of it. Doing fine. I spent the afternoon with them, told them to let me know if they needed any more help."

"It's good to see them really settling in, isn't it?"

"Yeah," Ben smiled. "They're really shaping up."

He got up and started toward the bedroom, pausing by the closed door to the storeroom. "So if you don't need me..."

"You should get some sleep," said Violet. "You really look exhausted."

He looked away from the storeroom door. "Yeah," he agreed. "I ought to get some sleep."

Ben kept an eye on his office door (closed) while he drank his coffee (tepid) and waited for the clerk to come back on the televideo line. It didn't take as long as he'd expected. It must be a quiet day over at the Retropolis Academy for the Unusually Inventive.

"No Doctor Sheckley. I mean, there *was* a Doctor Sheckley. He was granted a doctorate sixty-three years ago. But sixty-three years..."

That was far beyond the average life expectancy for a District scientist. Ben thanked the clerk and hung up.

The Registry offices were still quiet. He'd conferred with Violet very early in the morning, and they'd divided the tasks between them. He was to research Doctor Sheckley and follow Officer Arriaga, when she appeared, while Violet was to remain hidden at Ben's apartment. She'd try to learn what could be learned about the Technological Investment and Benevolent Licensing Company and their motive for buying a laboratory for a doctor who, as it turned out, didn't exist.

"He sure gets a lot of mail for an imaginary fella," Ben mused. And that gave him an idea. Who was reading Doctor Sheckley's mail?

He opened his office door and wandered outside. "Anybody see Arriaga this morning?"

Of the few who were in, nobody had. "Fearn? Rocklynne?"

No more luck there. Well, they'd been doing fine with their Code Red, and they knew where to find him.

"Big meeting with the Registrar this afternoon," Investigator Repp reminded him. "They should all be here then."

Unless they're smart enough to avoid big meetings, Ben thought. But they were still pretty new. They'd probably be there. Of course Rocklynne and Fearn might have too much on their hands to make it. *Lucky them.*

Violet's research had also gone well. The Technological Investment and Benevolent Licensing Company was a brand-new entity, one that was owned by another brand-new company which had been set up by a company that had recently been acquired by another brand-new company. *That* company listed Registrar Cartier as its managing director. If that seemed sloppy to Violet, she had to admit that anybody without her extensive connections would have had a lot more trouble untangling such a tangled mess of ownership.

So Registrar Cartier had set Doctor Sheckley up in business.

As to what that business was, she knew that Sheckley had not filed any preliminary or final patent applications; but he (or she) was taking correspondence from at least one firm of probate attorneys.

Violet had just mounted her attack on the court system when she hung up the phone to listen. Someone was coming down the hallway.

Silently, she rose from her chair and looked around Ben's apartment. There wasn't any place to hide. There were the usual closets, his bedroom, the arch that led to the kitchen; there were the usual facilities. But no place where a robot could conceal herself. Except for the storeroom.

She glided over to the closed storeroom door and tried the handle: locked. This didn't surprise her very much; Ben had been evasive about that room, after all. But she'd watched her locksmith companion very carefully when he opened the Registrar's door.

One piece of wire held the lock's wards, one by one, while she worked the other wire to pry them out of the way. She could hear somebody doing the exact same thing to the apartment's front door.

But Violet was a good observer. *Her* lock clicked open first. She darted inside, closing and locking the door again behind her.

It was dark, inside the storeroom. And if that other person was able to pick one lock, well…

Violet heard the apartment door open.

…a second lock wouldn't be much of a barrier. She turned, her eye lamps brightening, to see if there was anything in the room that could conceal her.

And, having turned, Violet could only stare.

"Have you seen Violet this morning?"

Ben looked up to see the cheerful face of the Registrar. He'd been going through some records, just on a hunch, and hadn't heard the boss at his door.

"Violet? No, I don't think so. Not today."

The Registrar paused, and looked a little less cheerful for a moment. "That's not like her," he said at last.

Ben agreed.

"I wonder, could she be staying at your apartment? For any reason?"

That was surprising. Maybe it shouldn't be.

"My *apartment?* No. Why? She's never been there."

"Just wondering where she might be. She, ah, she doesn't answer at home."

Ben figured he'd better stop that idea right away.

"No, she's never come by. And anyway, there's my cousin."

"Your…?"

"He should have come into the station about…" Ben looked at the clock. "Oh, about twenty minutes ago. He's got the key." He grinned, like he'd had a wonderful idea. "Hey, if she does come by, he's sure to see her. Should I call?"

"No, no, that's not, ah, not necessary. Just let me know if you hear from her, investigator."

The Registrar hurried out of Ben's office.

"Just a Scratch" BUT!
INFECTION IS AVOIDED
BY IMMEDIATE FIRST
TO-DAY

Violet had listened while the intruder walked into the bedroom, the kitchen, and the facilities. The intruder's footsteps were now coming straight at the door to what Ben had called his storeroom.

The footsteps stopped when the phone rang.

She heard the intruder step toward the phone, and whatever showed on the screen caused him (or her) to answer. Violet listened, but through the door she couldn't really hear the conversation: just two voices, muttering.

Whatever it was, the intruder fled the apartment. Violet heard the entry door's lock click back into place. Then she waited for five minutes.

She unlocked the door. When it swung open the light flowed into Ben's hidden room and revealed all its secrets. She looked around with two waves of powerful feelings crashing and breaking and swelling again, and again, two huge waves at war across the ocean of her circuits. One wave was pity; the other, terror.

It was a tough room. The investigators hadn't forgotten their last meeting, the one when they realized that they were all doing double duty for the same old pay; so they weren't very receptive to the Registrar's suggestion that they tell everybody they met how much they loved their Info-Slates.

Nobody challenged him, but there was sullen mutiny in the air.

Investigator Rocklynne was there, but apart from a terse "Fearn's handling it," he didn't comment on the Code Red that was trying to eat the world. Officer Arriaga came in late and sat in the back.

After the meeting Ben followed Officer Arriaga as she made her rounds. Those rounds included the laboratory of Doctor Sheckley, to which she had a key. She stayed inside for a few minutes and when she came out again she was carrying a stack of paperwork. The papers didn't look like patent applications.

Ben was pretty sure that they were legal documents, but he had no idea what kind of documents they might be. There wasn't a subtle way to find out, either. So at the end of the day he made his way home, keeping an eye on the reflections as he went. Nobody seemed to be following him.

He felt relieved and happy when he opened the door to his apartment to see Violet talking on the videophone. Then he saw that the studio door was standing open.

Violet's enameled head turned toward him. "Yes," she said. "We'll need to talk about that. Just let me finish up here."

She turned back to the videophone and Ben sank deep into the cushions on his couch.

He'd always feared this. He'd never really believed that it would happen. But here they were.

Ben's studio had no windows. The far wall was dominated by a gigantic drawing board; layers of drawings were taped there, haphazardly, each diagram or elevation view covering most of the one below. A little cabinet to the side held his pencils, pens, and three bottles of ink in different colors. The carpet around the tall stool was stained with all three of those colors and a few more, besides. Old puddles of coffee had dried and dyed the surface of the cabinet, but the parts of the drawing board that could still be seen were white and unmarked.

Every other wall was covered in dark wooden cabinets, with flat file drawers below and hinged frames above. The frames sat ten layers deep and were hinged so that they could fold out, like wings, to display dozens of drawings. When closed, they formed anonymous boxes that gave no clue to what the layers contained.

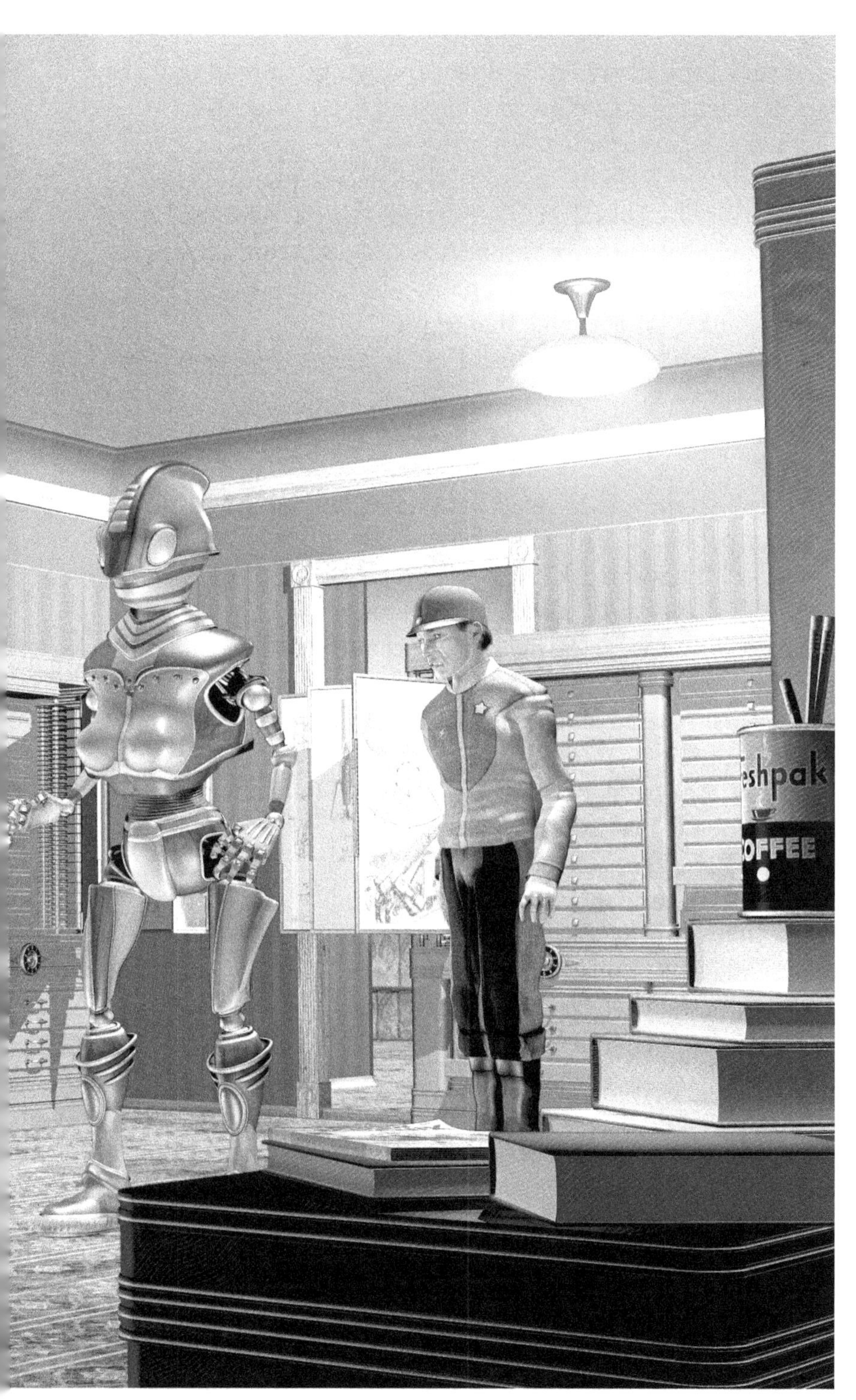
eshpak
COFFEE

Every cabinet was now open: the wings, spread out like murder victims on a clinical table, had been autopsied.

"I, uh, I can explain..."

"They speak for themselves," Violet said quietly. "The Reciprocating Ore Dissolver is very good, I think. And the Heat-Energized Moisture Converter. And the Towering Burrowing Pummelizer, which, well, the name –"

"I drank a lot of coffee that night."

"Yes. I see. A lot of coffee. How long has this been going on?"

Ben waved at the ranks of cabinets. "You know, for a while."

It felt strange, to have all his secrets laid open in front of another person. In front of *Violet*.

"And... I have to ask... the prototypes?"

"No! I never *built* any of them. That would... you know I can't do that. I can't *make* any of these things. Then I'd be a *scientist*. It's just, you know, when I can't stand it any more, when I just have to let some of the ideas out, then, you know, I come in here. And I draw the plans."

They looked at the drawing board. The drawings were half an inch thick, in some places.

"Oh, Ben."

"I've got it under control. It's a *system*."

"You're running out of space in the cabinets."

"Yeah. I, uh, I need to expand a little."

They stood there for a minute or two.

"Every night?" she asked.

Ben looked away. "Lately, yeah, well, it's been hard. With all the, you know, with the situation at the office. So, yeah, lately it's pretty much every night. Not *last* night. But most nights."

Violet remembered how he'd lingered at the studio door before he'd gone to bed. "Because I was here last night."

"Can we get out of here? I just, it's so...."

Violet led him out to the couch, and they sat. But she'd

left the studio door open, with the lights on in there.

"Do you ever wish you'd stayed in school? Become a scientist?"

"Oh, no. Never. I didn't want that kind of life. I couldn't... no. Never."

"But part of you wants it."

"Not... not *wants*. I just have to blow off some steam, sometimes. It's like the pressure builds up, and I have to turn the valve. For a little while."

They sat there, facing the studio door, and after a moment Violet's hand crept over to his.

"I understand," she said. "I really do."

And she did. She really did. But there wasn't much she could do about it.

It hadn't ever occurred to Violet that humans might resemble robots in this way: that they might have an overwhelming need to fulfill a particular role, or purpose, and that this need might be strong enough to force them into its service. She'd been built to the exact specifications for a secretary–and she was a *very good* secretary–but something had gone wrong, somewhere, so that her inbuilt purpose was to investigate: to examine, to question, and to worry away at the false information that obscured the facts; to find those facts, and to see that they were known.

Nothing else could satisfy her. Not really. No matter how often she insisted she'd set those hopes aside, she would never be content until she'd become the creature that she already was, inside. She *was* an investigator. It was just difficult to convince the world that this, so obvious to her, was true.

And Ben... she gave his hand a squeeze. Ben had taken a good look at what the world had in mind for him, and he had decided he wasn't going to go along with the world's plan. He'd simply refused. He had reinvented himself. He'd found another way to use his inborn skills, and he'd made a good life for himself as a patent investigator. But he couldn't change who he was inside, any more than Violet could. And if he'd made a choice that was different from the choice she'd made, it was still *his* choice.

She looked up at the open doorway to his studio, lined as it was with the dreams and compulsions to which he would not–not *completely*–surrender.

"Well," she said at last. "Every day's a battle for us, isn't it?"

Then she got up, and switched off the studio light, and closed the door.

"Doctor Sheckley is a professional heir," she said. "In the past three months Doctor Sheckley has inherited 242 patents from scientists who have failed to survive their research. And it's not just any research: in every case, the patents were for processes or devices that had commercial applications, *lucrative* applications. Doctor Sheckley is a very wealthy–"

"–imaginary person." Ben was still sunk deep in the couch, but now he looked up. "There is no Doctor Sheckley, Violet. He (or she) is a shell. A front. An illusion."

She nodded, slowly. She explained that the Technological Investment and Benevolent Licensing Company was, likewise, a shell, and that it was owned by Registrar Cartier.

She began to feel as though they'd found the facts, and that the facts were known. Most of them, anyway. And even though she and Ben were probably in danger she felt a soft glow of satisfaction creep through her circuits.

"He wants to run the Registry like a business. Like *his* business. And now we know how he plans to make it profitable."

"On the backs of dead inventors."

It was a gruesome thought.

"And Investigator Bok...."

"She was talking about forming a union, which would cut into his profits. And a union would keep a close eye on what he was doing, and how he was doing it, too."

Something about this still didn't make sense to Violet. "He'd have to get around City Government," she said. "Somehow, he'd have to turn the Registry into a commercial enterprise."

"Would he, though? The way he's set up Doctor Sheckley, the money still rolls in. Even if we're still a public agency."

It would work for him either way, she realized.

"We need to find Investigator Bok. And we need to stop the Registrar."

Ben nodded. She knew this was obvious. What was less obvious was how they were going to manage both of those things.

But two people who could reinvent themselves weren't likely to be put off by *that* kind of problem. They'd just have to find a way.

Ben waited with Grace Keaton under the trees on the west side of the Registry of Patents. They'd arrived separately–Ben on foot, Miss Keaton on her Aeroflite scooter–but, if all went well, they'd be leaving together.

You'd hardly know that the city was all around them, in their green-tinted pool of shadow and quiet. Ben could just hear the early morning crowd beyond the trees.

"So Violet had some kind of offer for you?" he asked.

The courier nodded. "Collection from an old, closed-down library. Newspapers, documents. Sold to a private collector about eighty-five years ago. She can get me access, she says."

Old newspapers and documents? It seemed like a strange desire, in a courier, and Ben said so.

"I'm a graduate student," she told him. "Looking for research materials for my dissertation."

"Which is about...?"

"Early history of Retropolis."

"Really? There's a lot of mystery there? I mean, everybody knows, you know...."

Miss Keaton grunted. "Everybody knows a kind of fairy tale. When you start really looking, there's almost no documentation for how the city started. What really happened."

Well. History. Ben guessed it was just the thing, for some people.

"Nice that Violet could help," he said.

"She seems to know a lot of people."

Ben knew that was true. He'd seen, over and over, how Violet could locate just about anyone who had, or did, or *could* do almost anything; and there was always another thing *that* person wanted, and Violet could find that, or someone who had it, and then....

"There she is," Miss Keaton said. "And about time, too. I still need to make my deliveries."

Violet, just back from the Probate Courts, had returned with a stack of wills and court filings that revealed how Doctor Sheckley had become the heir to a large number of District scientists, most of whom were already dead at the time their wills were filed.

"Someone's looking into it over there," she finished. "But it's likely to take them some time to follow the trail."

"You told them about the Technological Investment and Benevolent Licensing Company?"

"Yes. But they have to find the proof for themselves. They won't just take my word for it."

That was fair enough, Ben supposed, but Investigator Bok was still a problem: the prosecutors wouldn't be too concerned about a missing person when there was all that fraud right in front of them.

"So we go ahead with the plan," he said, and Violet nodded.

"Great," said Miss Keaton. "Let's get on with that, then."

Ben collected himself and thought through the steps of their plan. "Right. I'll go in and drop a hint, then. And,

Violet? You should probably go back to my apartment until this blows over."

Miss Keaton and Violet watched him as he headed for the Registry's side door.

"What are you *really* going to do?" the courier asked.

Violet bobbed her painted head. "Something else," she said, and she set off between the trees.

The odd thing was, when Ben passed Investigators Rocklynne and Fearn he could have sworn he heard them talking about Violet. But that was probably natural: everyone in the office must be wondering where she was. He didn't take the time to ask them about it, or about their progress on that Code Red. They were hurrying one way while he pretended not to hurry in another. It looked like they were headed back to the District.

There was a new secretary at Violet's desk, somebody from the pool. With that, and the absence of the coffee pot, Ben had a strange sense that he was in an unfamiliar place.

He looked at the closed door to the Registrar's office. This was Step One.

"He in?"

The new secretary nodded. "Yes, he came in early this morning. Was there something?"

"He ought to know that Investigators Rocklynne and Fearn are working a Code Red. Could be a bad one."

The look on her face told Ben that the secretary knew how bad a *bad* Code Red might be. "I'll tell him right away."

Ben waited for her to go through the door, and made sure she hadn't closed it.

Violet had given him a diagnostic code for the videophone. He stepped around the desk and dialed it, waited, and then he jumped when the phone rang, even though he'd placed the call himself.

"I'll get it," he called through the door, and he picked it up. There was just the quiet hiss of static on the line.

"No, it's Investigator Bowman," he said. He'd pitched his voice to carry. Then: "Bok? Hannah Bok? I thought you were on vacation."

Something fell over in the Registrar's office.

"Investigator Bok?" Ben continued, even louder. "I can't hardly hear you. Can you speak up?"

He timed it so that he was hanging up the phone just when Registrar Cartier came tumbling through the door. Ben shook his head. "Terrible connection," he said. "It was Investigator Bok, but I couldn't tell what she wanted."

He shrugged in the direction of the secretary. "Sorry."

"I'll call maintenance," the secretary said. "The lines must be acting up. But I was just telling the Registrar about your Code Red–"

The Registrar was staring at the videophone. "Yes. That sounded serious," he said in a faint voice.

Ben smiled. "They're on it, sir. Those new investigators, they're really shaping up. I'll check on them later, but I think they'll put a stop to it before the end of the day."

"Yes. That's fine, just fine. That's...."

After a moment, Ben decided that they weren't going to hear what that was. "Yeah, well, if there isn't anything else...?"

"Is Officer Arriaga in the building? I'd like to speak to her," said the Registrar.

"She's in the break room," his secretary said. "I'll go fetch her."

Ben smiled all the way out of the building. He was ready for Step Two.

The Aeroflite scooter is a useful vehicle, a favorite of couriers. It's fast, light, and has useful attachments, like the cargo trailer. The scooter's seat, though, isn't really built for more than one.

So Ben sat in the trailer.

This wouldn't have been his first choice. The wind was tugging at his uniform cap in the same way that it tugs at the ears of a Golden Retriever. But at least Miss Keaton hadn't picked up her packages for the District scientists. Ben didn't have to worry about what he was sitting on.

They'd only been circling the Registry for a minute or two when Ben spotted Officer Arriaga rushing out of the doors.

"That's her there," he said, and he pointed her out.

"Got her."

Miss Keaton glided above while Officer Arriaga hurried toward her destination. Ben was looking forward to seeing where that was, in Step Three.

Violet came into the Registry through the front door, exactly as though she owned the place. Plenty of people were glad to see her back. She let them know that she was glad to see them, too, and she continued to let them know all up and down the hallway outside the Registrar's office. She caught a glimpse of a strange secretary at her desk, and this bothered her more than she would have expected.

But, more importantly, Registrar Cartier saw *her*.

She took her time; she had to be sure that he was going to do something about it. But with Officer Arriaga out of the office she was pretty sure that the Registrar would need to handle her by himself.

While Ben had *been* flown over Retropolis before, he had never flown himself. You just didn't need to, with the monorails, the airships, the Transport Tubes (which no one really used, any more), the air taxis, and all the other forms of public transportation. If you lived within thirty miles of the place where you worked, as most people did, there wasn't any reason to own your own rocket. Or so Ben believed.

So Ben was an experienced passenger. He'd been practicing passengering all his life. Although it's not the kind of skill you brag about, and although, in fact, Ben had never thought about it much before today, he knew just about everything you needed to know about going for a ride while someone else did the flying. Or so Ben had believed.

But riding in the cargo cart behind Grace Keaton's scooter would test the skill and dedication of any passenger, regardless of experience; riding in that cargo cart was an entirely new form of transportation that, Ben felt, was never likely to become popular.

These were the things that Ben considered in between the breathtaking dives and the heart-stopping stalls, in those moments when the scooter hovered, briefly, under the overhang of a monorail pylon, or idled, also briefly, between the towers of one of the monumental buildings that carved canyons out of the city's skyline.

The rest of the time Ben's thoughts were completely nonverbal. Inasmuch as you could tell, these thoughts concerned the certainty of death.

"You okay back there?" Grace called.

"Mmmhnbkay."

"Good, that's great. May get a little rough up ahead."

Ben nodded. He didn't care whether she could see him.

Far below, he could see Officer Arriaga's uniform cap gliding up the escalator of a monorail pylon. He was pretty sure that the rest of Officer Arriaga was still underneath it.

"We'll need to keep up with that train, and watch to see who gets off at every station. Right?"

Ben gathered up what he could remember of human language. "Yep, watch the platforms, got it."

"They don't really go that fast," Grace offered. "But we need to pace them from above or below, to stay out of sight."

TIME MUSEU

"You do this a lot?"

"No, this is my first time. It's kind of interesting."

Well, Ben reasoned, *she spends her days flying around in a neighborhood where experiments are looking for new ways to kill her on every side and underneath. This might be sort of like a vacation to Grace.*

"There she goes," he said. "Green line, headed west."

Grace bent low over her handlebars. "Train number 20661," she replied. And they were off again.

Mostly, this was better. Grace would pick a spot that was invisible from the monorail windows and, like she said, the trains didn't go fast enough to challenge the little scooter. Things got a little exciting around the pylons, and at times when the architecture of the buildings around the tracks got really creative. Once they had to climb rapidly to avoid a little flock of ornithopters. The mechanical birds got interested and followed them at a safe distance, mirroring Grace's dips and turns. Ben turned around and watched the flock until Grace killed the rear jets and hovered above a sculpted eagle's head that jutted out, like a huge gargoyle, from the side of a building.

The train paused while passengers debarked. Ben and Grace peered down at the tops of their heads. There wasn't a Registry cap among them.

By the time the train got going again, the ornithopters had gotten interested in the eagle's head. Grace pulled away from the building and Ben watched the flock hover in place, waiting for the eagle to do something. He waved goodbye.

Three stops later, they saw Officer Arriaga exit the train onto a platform and start down the escalator.

This was a difficult moment. The monorail station had exits on every side, so they had to circle it quickly if they were going to see which way the officer was headed. Grace, by necessity, was watching ahead, so Ben concentrated on the rest of the train platforms. If Arriaga were to change trains somewhere on the lower levels they might lose her. The scooter was high enough that you couldn't identify them from below, but of course that meant it was hard to see who was coming through the doors down on the ground. So their two pairs of eyes were pretty busy, and Ben, at least, was worried.

"There she goes," he heard Grace say, and the cart leaped when the scooter suddenly dipped down and swooped north. Ben hung on and gritted his teeth.

They continued to shadow the officer, hugging the cover of the skyways and buttresses, while she walked through the trees between the buildings and crossed the wandering pathways of the park at Shulba Circle. Then Grace dove swiftly down.

Officer Arriaga had entered the main doors at Tubular Belle's.

"You're looking for a missing person, right?"

Ben nodded. "That's right."

"Well, then this is interesting," Grace said. She set the scooter down across the way from Tubular Belle's hotel.

Ben hopped out of the cart, a little unsteady but happy to feel the ground under his feet. He looked up at the building's tiled walls. There weren't many windows, here at Belle's.

"If you, uh, just wait here, I'll follow her in," he said.

"Yep. I'll be waiting." She was tying the scooter to the cleats in the ground.

Ben hurried across the grass toward the doors.

"Good luck!" Grace called from behind him.

Registrar Cartier spent most of his time behind a desk. Well, so did Violet, of course: but a robot can sit on chairs all day long without beginning to spread over them, the way human people do. So Violet had no trouble staying ahead of the Registrar when she left the Registry and set off across the city. He had certainly taken the bait.

It would have been convenient to take the monorail, but

SPACE HELMETS - AIR TANKS - RAY GUNS - RADIOS
MAGNETIC BOOTS - COMPASSES - SLIDE RULES

A Fine Selection
of Equipment & Supplies
to Meet the Exacting
Requirements of all
your Undertakings

All Sales Guaranteed
Now in stock: Aero-Vac Helmets!

O'MALLEY'S ADVENTURE OUTFITTERS
THE MAIN MONORAIL TERMINAL - SEVENTH FLOOR

AN ADVENTURE FOR EVERYONE'S BUDGET

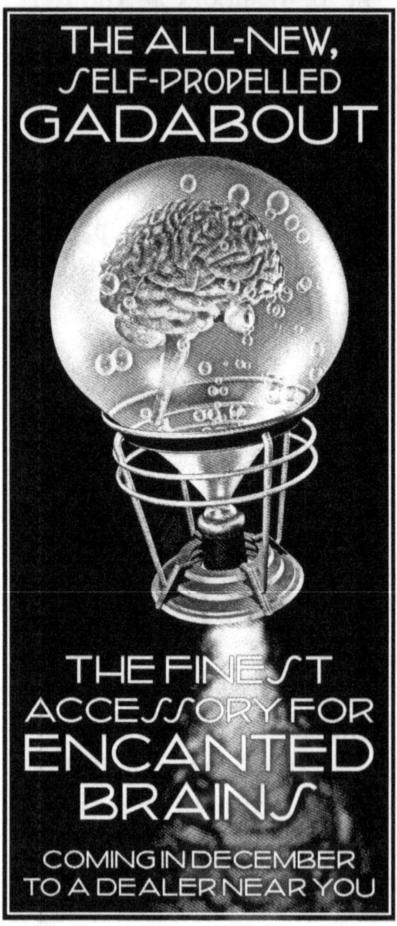

THE PODS OF THE TUBE TRANSPORT SYSTEM

Not as Bad as you Think!

private, personal
direct, speedy, exciting

RETROPOLIS
TRANSIT AUTHORITY

she didn't want to find herself in a train car with him. So she bustled on ahead of Registrar Cartier and made her way on foot.

She could track the man's progress in the windows and glassy walls of most buildings, until she crossed a walkway that was, sadly, going brown and sere due to its proximity to the Experimental Research District. Once in the District her feet rang on the pavement, echoing from wall to wall, because you just didn't get greenbelts in there. They always died, or turned into something else, and when it came right down to it the scientists in the District really didn't care.

The neighborhood was also short on windows and reflective surfaces, its architecture being more skewed toward the durable than the attractive. So Violet wasn't exactly sure how close the Registrar was, any more. She picked up her pace. She had no plans to talk to the man until she'd got where she was going.

As she passed the corner of Hydraulic Overflow and Palpitation Court she caught a glimpse of Investigators Rocklynne and Fearn. Fearn spotted her and raised four fingers on one hand, then held up her wrist watch with the other. Without returning Fearn's look, Violet bobbed her head. She turned onto Palpitation Court and approached the cul-de-sac at its end. She was walking quite slowly, now.

Palpitation Court ended at the laboratory of Doctor Schoen, an unremarkable bunker of the usual design except for its extended upper floor; this hung over the cul-de-sac in an arrangement of fire escapes that were quite interesting, in their way, a way which expired after a minute and a half of Violet's observation of them.

She turned at last, slowly and dramatically.

Registrar Cartier still hadn't arrived.

He'd been sitting behind a desk for a long time.

So she waited, gradually becoming concerned about the silent countdown that was running in her head, until the Registrar puffed around the corner and came to a sudden stop.

"Hello, Registrar."

"Violet."

He started walking toward her, clutching his briefcase.

"You should have let Officer Arriaga catch you," he said. "She was only going to take you off to a nice, long sleep. As it is..."

He opened the briefcase, and drew out a long, wicked-looking ray gun.

"...this will be much less pleasant. And more permanent."

Violet's eyes swung from his mustache, which was always distracting, to the barrel of the gun.

Ben's eyes fastened on the concierge at the front desk of Tubular Belle's. He was about to ask if she'd seen Officer Arriaga when the concierge smiled and greeted him. "You must be looking for Miss Belbas."

That settled that, then. Calliope Belbas was definitely the same person as Officer Arriaga.

"It's the uniform, right? Which way did she go?"

"Corporate Accounts, 12C," the concierge told him. "I must say, I was surprised to see her come back so soon."

"So...."

"Well, she's a resident, of course."

"She, uh, maybe she came back for something."

The concierge's face froze for a moment. Then she laughed.

Ben realized his mistake. "Yeah. My little joke."

He followed her directions to the elevator and punched the 'up' button.

On the twelfth floor, he found a map with the corporate halls mapped out. 12C was rented to the United City Expansion and Prosperity Corporation, no doubt one of the Registrar's many business enterprises. On either side of the map, and indeed stretching out along the halls in every direction, were the tubes.

Some people looked down on the residents of Tubular Belle's. But the way Ben saw it, the place was a pretty practical approach to living space. More living than space, naturally, and in fact more sleeping than living. But if you don't need to have a lot of stuff around you then the tubes at Belle's made a lot of sense. Most of the tubes near Ben were open and empty, but there were a few that were still occupied.

Each tube was about eight feet long (to allow for the equipment) and about two feet in diameter. They slanted up from the floor on track supports. On the bases were dials and gauges and levers. While in use, the tubes were lit up within with a soft, blue glow that really didn't flatter the faces of the occupants. But they were asleep. They didn't care.

When you rented a tube at Belle's, you returned to it at bedtime. You stepped up into your tube; you set the duration of your sleep; you pressed a button; and then it was tomorrow, or next week, or next year. Belle's had all kinds of long-term rates. People said the sleep was very refreshing. And the tubes acted as soniclaves, too, so when you woke up you and your clothes had been cleaned while you slept.

If it hadn't been for the space he needed for his studio, Ben figured that Belle's might be just the place for him.

As he walked toward section 12C, Ben passed a small, stooped man who'd brought his cart to a stop next to one of the tubes.

"'Morning," Ben said, and the man jumped.

"Uh, sorry."

The little man barely looked at him; he was also not looking at the underlit, blue-glowing face of the tube's resident.

"I guess you didn't hear me walking up."

The little man turned his back on the glowing tube. "I try to... to be someplace else when I'm working," he explained. "They're just so... so *blue*."

The tube-dwellers were pretty blue, due to the lighting in the tubes. Ben guessed they might get on your nerves. "Worked here long?"

"Fourteen years." The man whipped around, glaring (for once) at the sleeper in the tube. It was like he was trying to catch the tube-dweller staring at his back.

"Um, okay," Ben told him. "You know where 12C is?"

The man shuddered and pointed, but of course Ben already knew where it was. "Anybody else just come through here? In a uniform like mine?"

"12C–28 was just here," the man said. "Going that way."

He started to clean the glass tube with a spray bottle and a towel.

"Okay, then. Thanks."

Ben was still shaking his head when he rounded the corner to section 12C.

There was Officer Arriaga, checking the dials on a tube. Ben looked up at the tube and saw the eerie, blue-lit face of Investigator Bok.

She wasn't alone. There were at least a dozen other sleepers in the 12C tubes, several of them in the livery of the Zoning Department.

Ben started to say "Huh," but Officer Arriaga had come off the floor like a spring, her fist aimed at his face and her left lag pivoting around in the beginning of a roundhouse kick that Ben expected to really, really hurt until her fist connected and he stopped thinking about anything at all.

In spite of his slow progress on the way here, the Registrar had pulled out his pistol a little early. She hadn't expected the pistol at all, honestly. Violet counted off the seconds in her enameled head and tried to think of a way to delay him.

"Ben will have found Hannah Bok by now," she said. "And the courts are suddenly very curious about you."

"There's nothing for them to find," he said. "And your allegations about Investigator Bok are a bit desperate, aren't they?"

They were, she knew. A *little* desperate. But, still, he was wrong about the first thing.

"The Technological Investment and Benevolent Licensing Company," she said. "The Apogee Financial Advisory Service. The Convergence Trust. Ley, Jameson, and Simak, Attorneys at Law. Gallun, Tanner, and Manning (also Attorneys at Law)..."

The gun barrel twitched, just a little.

"...and Doctor Sheckley, of course."

"How did you...?"

"Just a bit of investigating, Registrar. You may think you've been clever, but it's all there, obvious to anybody who looks closely."

"So it was Ben Bowman, then."

"No, Registrar. Ben's always very helpful and supportive, but this was me. The one who exposed you, I mean. The one who ruined your plans. It's me."

The seconds were still ticking by. The gun barrel hadn't dropped.

Investigators Rocklynne and Fearn came around the corner behind the Registrar, quietly, and gestured at Violet. But it was still too soon.

"What *are* you?" the Registrar wondered.

And that was a good question, but now it was time. Violet sprang back toward the door to the laboratory and landed nimbly on the steps just as Doctor de Camp's circle of nothingness swept along the street and came to a stop, almost directly under the Registrar.

He looked very surprised when he dropped out of this world and into another one.

The two investigators and Violet stepped up to the edge of the hole.

"If it hadn't been for the gun," said Investigator Fearn, "I'd have said we should get him out of there."

Investigator Rocklynne agreed. "He really shouldn't have pulled a gun."

They could hear the Registrar screaming, fifteen feet and a universe away. Somewhere, much more distant, they heard an answering roar.

Only a fool, thought Violet, *brings a gun to a Science fight.*

Well, that was stupid, Ben thought. *I should have brought a gun or something.*

He'd woken in just about the worst position he could imagine, slumped halfway out of one of Belle's glass tubes and sort of upside down, with his feet dangling over the control panel and his face pressed into the blue light in the tube's base. His everything hurt. He slid out and backwards until he collapsed on the floor.

Something was going on.

He turned toward the rhythmic slamming sound that was making his brain hurt, only to find that it was someone else's brain that was under attack.

Officer Arriaga/Calliope Belbas was flat out on the floor, unconscious. The strange tube cleaner had the business end of a push broom pressed into her throat, and he was hitting her in the head, over and over, with a bucket.

"Buddy, I think you got her," said Ben. "Ease up a little."

The little man's blazing eyes fixed on him. "It's true!" he sputtered. "I *knew* they were trying to convert us. I knew it! They come out of their tubes, and the next thing you know they're coming for us. If I'd been a minute later, she'd have turned it on and you'd be blue, just like them!"

He was still hitting her, Ben noticed, so slowly he pulled himself up and dragged himself over to them. He took the bucket away.

"Look, I'm pretty sure this whole section is going to get

woken up today. So that's like, a big win for our side, right? For the non-blue. Uh, what a victory."

He set the bucket down out of the little man's reach. "Do you have something we can use to tie her up? She's a feisty one."

He took the push broom, which he considered a really good idea, and kept it pressed into her throat. "Some rope, or some packing tape, or something," he suggested.

The wild-eyed cleaner was happy to oblige.

When Ben got back to the Registry it had been overrun by people from the courts, and from City Government, and probably from some other places. He was giving all his attention to Officer Arriaga and he probably missed a few. She was awake now, and definitely not happy, maybe because Ben had sat on top of her in Grace's cart all the way back here; and before they left he'd loaded his pockets and the inside of his tunic with rocks, in the interest of ballast. Or so he'd explained to Grace. The courier seemed to revise her opinion of him after she saw him drag Officer Arriaga out of Belle's.

He didn't mention the cleaner. Best to keep it simple.

There was a whole lot of investigating going on, mainly in the Registrar's office, and the prosecutors were happy to take Officer Arriaga off his hands. "Calliope Belbas, or Officer Arriaga, or about four other names we know of," one explained. "Honestly, we don't know who she really is."

Ben had a feeling she wouldn't be very helpful with that, or with anything else. He explained about Section 12C at Belle's, and they sent someone to get those tubes opened.

As happy as the investigators were, though, they seemed pretty disappointed that no one knew where to find the Registrar. It turned out that they'd been investigating him over at the Zoning Department, and since it was so hard to prove their case against him they'd arranged his transfer to the

Patent Registry to get him out of the way.

The chief prosecutor explained. "Nobody actually wanted the job. For some reason Patent Registrars always seem to disappear, or get arrested, or to have a personal emergency and retire. The word's out, I mean. We're going to have a terrible time, finding you a new one."

It was about then that Violet returned to the office. She called Ben aside. "Rocklynne and Fearn should have that Code Red straightened out this afternoon," she told him. "They've got every scientist on the street working on it. Once they've extracted his atmosphere, Doctor De Camp and his invention ought to...."

"Yeah, that should do it," Ben agreed. "But... wait... when did you run into them?"

The prosecutor was still apologizing about how hard it would be to get a new Registrar.

"I have an idea," Violet said. "You could make a temporary appointment, say, just to keep things running smoothly. You could promote someone from within."

The prosecutor called one of the City Government people over. "Did you hear that? We could find somebody who's already here, and, uh, not concerned about the thing with the Registrars. The history, I mean. As an interim appointment."

City Government liked that idea. "Who's that investigator that broke the case? The one who exposed Cartier and brought Belbas in?"

"That would be Ben Bowman," Violet said. "He's right here."

Ben grunted, but Violet's foot had settled on his. She could really get some compression going when she wanted to.

"Okay, you, Bowman. You're the Acting Registrar. Until we find a qualified candidate. All settled. Now can somebody find the Registrar we lost?"

"My office," Ben said to Violet. She moved toward the Registrar's door. "No. I mean the other one."

They made their way to Ben's – well, to Ben's *old* office

– and closed the door. A lot of conversation was going on outside.

"That was just mean," Ben said. "A *promotion*." He turned to face her. "They're not going to find Cartier, are they?"

She toyed with the coffee pot, but that was cowardly. So she looked up, and into Ben's eyes. "Doctor de Camp's experiment should be shut down now, so no. They won't find him."

"Oh."

"The last thing he said to me was 'What are you?' And I knew. I guess I knew all along. And *you* knew, of course."

They stood there by the door. They thought about it. Ben remembered those distant roars, and the strange green glow, and the fragments of Professor Kline that he'd stumbled over in the crystal cavern.

"I bet it's going to take them a long time to find a new Registrar," he said at last, and Violet agreed.

He walked over to the videophone and called Supplies. "Yeah, this is Bowman," he said.

"Congratulations, Registrar!"

"Um, yeah, thanks. That's just temporary. But I need an Investigator's badge, okay? Just send it up. A new one."

Violet stared at him. He stared back. Then she pulled the coffee out of his drawer and started to make a pot.

"You don't have to do that any more, Investigator," he said. "That's a secretary's job."

"Haven't you noticed? I'm versatile."

The pot began to bubble, softly, quietly, and they listened to it for awhile. It was soothing.

"You're going to have to get me out of this Registrar business, though."

"I will, Ben. I will."

MORE BOOKS BY BRADLEY W. SCHENCK

Slaves of the Switchboard of Doom (Tor Books, 2017)

The Lair of the Clockwork Book (2012 / 2017)

Trapped in the Tower of the Brain Thieves (2010)

Celtic Knotwork Borders in Repeating Sections (2007)

AND ON THE WORLD WIDE WEB

Webomator (www.webomator.com)

Retropolis (shop.webomator.com/retropolis)

Thrilling Tales of the Downright Unusual (thrilling-tales.webomator.com)

The Celtic Art Works (shop.webomator.com/celtic-art-works)

radioplanetbooks.com

www.ingramcontent.com/pod-product-compliance
Lightning Source LLC
Chambersburg PA
CBHW072259130726
47910CB00012B/2163

* 9 7 8 0 9 9 9 6 5 0 9 0 5 *